RUTHLESS QUEEN

Ruthless Royals Book Two

AMANDA RICHARDSON

Ruthless Queen
Amanda Richardson
Published by Amanda Richardson
© Copyright 2021 Amanda Richardson
www.authoramandarichardson.com

Editing by Traci Finlay
Cover Design by Moonstruck Cover Design & Photography

AUTHOR'S NOTE

Ruthless Queen is a high-school bully reverse harem romance. All characters are 18+. Please be sure you've read book one, Ruthless Crown, before diving into this one.

Please note the trigger warnings in the blurb, which is located on the next page.

Hunter, Ash, Ledger, and Samson.
The Kings of Ravenwood Academy.
Their names still send shivers down my spine, for more
than one reason.

Back then, they didn't expect me to fight back.
But I did.
And now I'm theirs.

After making a pact with them, they help me get revenge
on the one man who wronged me.
I'm not the same meek, little girl that got taken advantage
of.
Now, I have four ruthless guys willing to risk everything
for me.

The only problem is, I promised them everything I had in
return for their help.
So while I may be the new Queen of Ravenwood, the
Kings still own me, body and soul.

And I'm not quite sure I'm ready to hand over my crown.

Ruthless Queen is full-length high-school bully reverse
harem romance. It is book two of the Ruthless Royals
duet. It is advised to read them in order. *Please note
Ruthless Queen contains explicit language, bullying,
violence, and flashbacks of abuse/trauma. It also features
four hot AF guys who would do anything to protect their
feisty Queen. The story concludes with this book and does
have a HEA.

For all the ladies who've ever been shamed for reading romance.

Fuck the haters.

PROLOGUE

Nine months ago

The knife slices through the zucchini with ease, and I accidentally nick the tip of my left index finger.

"Shit," I whisper, setting the knife down and sucking on the cut. After pulling it out, the blood pools on my skin in a thick droplet, and I reach over for a paper towel. Just as I tear a piece off, a warm hand settles on my back.

"I'm fine," I tell Cam, shaking my finger. "Just a tiny cut." I twist around and look up at him, holding it up. "See?"

His face is oddly serious—his eyes narrowed.

"What?" I ask, turning back to dinner, but his other hand grips my wrist and tugs me into his body. I gasp. "What are you—"

"Shh," he whispers, his other hand reaching under my dress to caress my thigh.

Pure ice skims along the nape of my neck, and shivers claw down my spine, one vertebra at a time. My legs tremble as his hand does little circles on my skin, and then he sniffs my hair.

"Cam?" I ask, choking out a sob. His hand moves between my legs. I try to push him away, but he's so much stronger than me. "What—what are you doing?"

"I said be quiet," he snaps, bending down. His breath—hot and smelling of beer—churns my stomach. I tamp down the bile rising in my throat. "You think I don't know you wore this dress for me, pretty girl?"

I swallow, shaking. It's just a simple sundress—one I wear often.

I'm seventeen.

And you're dating my mom.

"No," I whisper, shaking my head vehemently. "No, I thought—"

"You want me," he growls, moving my underwear to the side. I stiffen when I hear him unzip his pants. "Be a good little girl and bend over."

I begin to cry. "No. Stop, please," I beg, squeezing my eyes closed as he turns me around and shoves me against the counter. I try to resist, but he has me pinned beneath him, his front to my back. The stone cuts into my stomach, and then I feel him push into me.

"Ow," I cry, tears leaking down my cheeks. "Please, stop."

You were supposed to be my friend. All these months, and you were supposed to be my friend. None of my mom's other boyfriends did this—and none of our interactions ever gave me any idea of what was to come.

.Of what's happening now.

A monster—he's a monster.

"Don't be stupid, pretty girl," he rasps.

I try twisting out of his grip, but he has both hands behind my back, and his large body has me pinned underneath him. I scream, but his hand comes to my mouth.

I try biting him, but his other hand slaps my face. His breathing quickens, and my stomach roils with nausea.

"You have such a tight, little pussy," he says, his voice menacing and cruel.

How can this be the same guy who taught me how to drive? How can this be the guy everyone loves, the one who wins good Samaritan awards, who everyone respects? Is it because he's been drinking? Is he on drugs?

"Cam," I cry, my voice breaking as I sob. "Why are you doing this?"

"You want me. You've always wanted me. You think I haven't noticed the way you wear those tight, little outfits around me? Always asking me if I want a beer? Inviting me over the minute your mom goes out of town?"

No. He has it all wrong. None of that was for him. And as for tonight, *he* asked what I was doing. I had no idea.

I thought we were friends.

I was trying to imagine what it would be like to have a father figure in my life—someone to protect me, someone to watch out for me, to eat dinner and watch a movie with me.

I scream again, and this time, he shoves my face into the counter. I feel blood trickling out of my nose as I try to move out of his grip.

He grunts, panting, and I know he's almost finished. I look to my right, at the kitchen knife lying on its side. I just need one free hand, one second to grab the handle...

"I'm coming," he whispers, and the revulsion powers through me.

I hate him.

For ruining his relationship with my mom—with me.

For *raping* me.

For reading everything all wrong, for assuming a teenager would be attracted to someone almost forty.

I grind my teeth as he finishes, and then a loud, shrill ring pierces through the air.

His phone.

He loosens his grip on my arms ever so slightly— enough for me to twist around and grab the knife off the counter, and suddenly the knife is an inch from his neck.

He gives me a cruel smile and slaps my hand away. It almost works.

Almost.

I bring my hand up again and plunge it into the side of his neck.

His eyes widen, and he screams as blood spurts out of his body. The ringing phone stops suddenly. Moving his hand to the injury, he stumbles backwards.

But it's too much blood.

He sways, looking at me with a stunned expression.

I fall back against the counter, the knife clattering to the ground as Cam drops to his knees.

His eyes pin me in place, a look of hatred on his face as they flutter closed and he falls over. The blood is beginning to seep through his T-shirt, forming a small pool beneath his body...

I killed him.

I killed him.

I killed him.

With the sliver of dignity that I have left, I pick up my phone and dial 9-1-1. I could leave him here to rot, but I'm not a monster like him. That would be too easy. When the operator answers, I quickly tell her that a man has been stabbed, and that he's losing a lot of blood.

Maybe he doesn't deserve it.

Maybe I should leave him to die.

Frowning, I step over his body, my legs still shaky and wobbly.

I open the sliding door to the back patio, opening the gate and weaving through the parking lot, to the edge of the forest.

I don't know where I'm going.

I just know I need to run.

1

BRIAR

Pretty girl...

I gasp as I sit up, the darkness of my bedroom surrounding me. Cam's voice is still ringing in my ears as I look around, my heart thumping against my chest heavily.

Still breathless, I close my eyes and place my hand on my neck, willing myself to get control of my breathing. The sheets are twisted around my body, so it takes a second to untangle myself. I throw my legs over the side of the bed and lean forward, resting my elbows on my bare thighs, breathing in deeply, exhaling slowly...

My throat feels like sandpaper—I need water.

I exit my room, padding down the stairs to the kitchen. Opening a cupboard, I pull a glass out and fill it up at the sink, which is quicker than using the fancy spout we have on the island sink.

Gulping deeply, I finish the glass and refill it, drinking that one, too.

It's been two weeks since Samson spotted Cam in the grocery store—two weeks since my stepbrother and his three friends became my biggest protectors.

Two weeks since we decided not to tell anyone he was in Greythorn.

Closing my eyes, I set the glass on the counter.

These two weeks feel like an eternity. I haven't had a restful night of sleep since before everything happened.

It's not a coincidence that he's here, but the fact that I have no idea what he's planning? It's terrifying, and those morbid thoughts keep me up most nights.

And we haven't been able to track him down.

He could be *anywhere*.

I walk back to my room, closing the door. When I turn around, I scream.

Someone is sitting in the chair, hidden in the shadows.

Waiting.

2

Hunter

"Sorry, didn't mean to scare you," I mutter, standing. "I heard you go downstairs, and I couldn't sleep."

She takes a deep breath, her hand coming up to her neck as she shakes her head.

"Fuck. I thought you were—"

"Briar." My voice is hard. "He can't get to you here." What I don't say is that this place is a fortress. After my dad found out about Cam escaping from San Quentin, he had more cameras installed outside the house, and a 24/7 security guard that roams the front of the house. No one is getting in here. We made sure of that.

"I don't trust him," she breaths. "He was a cop. He might know how to get around the alarm—"

"Briar," I mutter, walking over to her. She looks up at me, her grey eyes visible in the light of the window. There's a full moon tonight, and I know that has something to do with how spooked she is lately—especially given that Greythorn is in full-blown Halloween mode.

"He'll kill me," she whispers. "I know that's why he's here."

"Briar," I repeat, my voice soothing as I pull her into a tight hug. She relaxes instantly, exhaling loudly as I rub her back. "There's no point in worrying about this right now. You need to sleep."

I remember her first day at Ravenwood Academy—how her face had shown true fear when I grabbed her wrist. But this? This is different. This is her worst nightmare come alive, and I don't know what else I can do to reassure her, to make her feel safe.

Trying to find Cam—trying to hang around the store where Samson noticed him, asking around, keeping an eye out in town, stalking the local hotel, wandering around in hopes of running into him—has all led to nothing. Samson recounted his story a hundred times, trying desperately to hone in on any clues, but nothing ever came to fruition. We hit dead ends at every turn.

He'd seemingly disappeared overnight.

I know it bothers Briar that she has no idea if he went back to California, or if he's just biding his time and making plans. We don't know when or how he'll make himself known. It gives him an unfair advantage, and I know Briar feels like a caged animal because of it.

"I won't let anyone touch you," I murmur, tugging her into me. God, she's so warm and soft. And she smells so fucking good.

She nuzzles her face into my chest, and I take a steadying breath.

"I know."

She has me—she has *us*. Four of us, sworn to protect her.

Her body sags sleepily against mine, and I help her into bed, tucking the sheets around her body and then placing the thick duvet over her. She turns onto her side and curls into a ball, closing her eyes. All of this is getting to her—plus the fact that her friends aren't talking to her, and her mom is pregnant... It's a lot.

I sigh. "Cameron Young may think he's getting revenge on you, but we have the upper hand of knowing he's here. We can brace ourselves and plan to deploy our attack first," I murmur into her ear. "*We* have the control this time. And you have *all of us*."

"I just want it done already," she mumbles. "I want to move on."

"I know. It will be. Soon."

3

BRIAR

Scarlett and Jack walk right past me on the quad. Just as I'm about to call out to them, they disappear into the thick, grey fog, which settles over the entire campus at Ravenwood Academy. I watch as it slowly descends upon me, and as I turn around to walk back to the car, I suddenly can't breathe. I'm gasping for air, and one of my hands goes over my mouth as I try to outrun the heavy mist pressing down on my chest. Coughing, I look down at my hand, noticing the bright, red blood. As my pulse speeds up, I touch my neck and feel wetness. Thick blood is soaking my white button-up...

I scream, sitting up in bed. The early morning light is just beginning to peak through my curtains. Breathing heavily, I throw the covers off and stomp to the shower, turning it on and sitting on the toilet as I let it heat up.

I haven't had nightmares like this since I was a kid. Even when everything happened with Cam, I didn't have a single nightmare. I think knowing he had been arrested and couldn't get to me—couldn't seek revenge for what I did to him—was a comfort. As horrible as it all was, at least he was arrested and put in jail. At least he was contained, with security.

Or so I thought...

I step into the large, marble shower. Turning the brass fixture so that the water is scalding hot, I tilt my head back and get my hair wet, trying to dislodge the horror of my nightmare from my mind. I know I'm still processing everything—still coming to terms with Cam being in Greythorn. Even in sleep, I can't seem to find true peace.

Even in sleep, he haunts me.

And now he's here.

Waiting.

The thought sends shivers clawing down my spine, despite the warmth of the shower. I can't even call Sonya —and I really wish I could, because I need her more than ever right now—because I don't want anyone else to know that he's been spotted. Besides, she's only going to tell me it's an irrational fear—that just because he escaped prison on the other side of the country doesn't mean he's going to show up at my doorstep. *Oh, how wrong she would be.*

All the progress I've made these last nine months is falling to pieces, and the one person who helped me through my trauma can't even help me with this.

I wash and dry my hair, and then I get ready for the day. Zipping my skirt up, I pull on a pair of sheer black tights and step into my boots, the latter of which are against dress code.

Andrew, my stepfather and the headmaster of Ravenwood Academy, feels terrible about Cam escaping prison.

He's not going to say anything, even if he did care. In the grand scheme of things, it's such a small matter.

I tuck my white button-up into my skirt and place my hair into a high ponytail before heading downstairs. I smile when I hear voices, and as I round the corner of the staircase, I see Hunter, Ash, Ledger, and Samson all sitting with my mom and Andrew in the formal dining room.

"Morning, sweetie," my mom chirps, despite the decaf she's now drinking. I don't know how Aubrey Monroe gave up caffeine. She is way more of a coffee fiend than I am, and that's saying a lot. I guess pregnancy really does change your priorities.

"Hi," I answer, walking past them to the kitchen to make myself a latte. Just as I pull the espresso off the shelf, a warm hand settles on my back.

"I'll get it," Hunter mumbles, smiling down at me. His eyes darken as he takes in my outfit, and his hand reaches up to my ponytail, yanking ever so gently. "I like this. A lot," he growls.

My knees buckle and I swallow, pulling away. "Thanks," I say, nodding to the coffee he's making me.

He does this every morning. I slept in yesterday, and I was sure he was gone when I woke up past eleven, but just as I stepped into the kitchen, I heard him sauntering over from the library where he'd been writing. It's like he has antennas attached to his head that alert him whenever I need coffee.

We don't talk as the espresso sputters out. He foams my milk, and I pull my lower lip into my mouth as I look up at him, and he glances down at me with a lopsided smile.

"You naughty girl," he whispers, smirking.

Pouring the milk into my mug, he adds a couple pumps of vanilla—just the way I like it. Stirring gently, he hands it to me. "Voila," he jokes, ushering me back to the formal dining room.

I take a seat next to Ledger, and he winks at me. "Good morning, Briar," he purrs, placing some eggs, toast with butter, and bacon on my plate. "Would you like some sausage?" he asks, his eyes twinkling at the double entendre.

I wasn't prepared for these boys—wasn't prepared for how they'd all look in their uniforms, how the white button-ups would make them seem older, somehow. How Ledger's tongue ring catches the morning light, and I remember how it felt between my legs. As I glance around the table, I have to think of something else as I cross my ankles together—something to tamp down the potent need for them. They each unravel me in a distinctive way, each offering me something different. Once again, I'm baffled as to why they want to protect me when Cam is not their problem.

"How'd you sleep, Briar?" Andrew asks, smiling and handing me the jam.

Terrible.

I want to tell him—and my mom—about Cam. That he's here. But I don't. I'm not even sure the authorities could get to him. Where would they even begin to look? If he drove here from California and used cash, like I suspect...he's untraceable. And since he used to be a cop, I have a feeling he did everything in his power to stay under the radar.

No, it's better if my mom and Andrew don't know.

"Very well, thank you," I answer politely.

I can feel all their eyes on me—and then a hand on my knee. I jerk my head to the left, and Ash's lips twitch as his calloused fingers circle my kneecap, causing me to clench my legs together.

"I'm just so glad you've found a wonderful group of friends," my mom adds, smirking. She *must* have some idea. She hasn't said anything, but then again, she's in bed at seven most nights because of the pregnancy fatigue. "How are Scarlett and Jack doing?"

My mom doesn't know that either, of course. How could I explain that they're not speaking to me because I slept with three of the Kings, and fooled around with the fourth?

"They're good. Busy," I lie.

She smiles and shifts her gaze to my left. "And you're finding your room here to be okay, Ash?"

He nods. "Yes, ma'am."

Oh, he's good.

I sometimes forget that Ash lives here now, that we've sort of taken him under our wing because his father is in jail for child abuse. He gives her a charming smile and takes a sip of his black coffee, his teeth straight and white, with a dimple in one cheek that sort of takes the edge off his harsh and brutal demeanor. It was like the universe decided one hot housemate wasn't enough—now I have two.

"Samson was just telling us that he got early admittance to MIT," Andrew says proudly, clapping Samson on the back. I swear I see his cheeks redden slightly at the attention.

"Yeah," Samson says slowly, shrugging. "I found out this weekend."

"That's amazing news," I exclaim, grinning.

"Ash and Ledger both got letters from Harvard and Yale as well," Andrew continues. "Early conditional acceptances," he adds, beaming. When I look at the two of them, neither of them seems very excited. I wonder if this is their dream, or the expectation of attending a school like Ravenwood? "Ravenwood Academy truly is the best preparatory school around." Looking at me, he smiles even broader. "You'll have no problem attending any school in Paris, Briar."

Nervous, excited butterflies bounce through me. "I'm very excited to begin the application process," I answer, sipping my coffee as I ignore the guilt working through me.

Everything happening with Cam really throws a wrench into their futures, doesn't it? I feel like I can't ask for their help without returning the favor somehow, even though returning the favor isn't or wasn't ever expected of me. But Hunter is well on his way to becoming America's next greatest writer, and now Samson, Ash, and Ledger have early acceptances to world renowned universities. They have futures to protect, reputations, money...

Them getting mixed up with me—and everything from my past—could jeopardize everything they've worked their whole lives toward.

"I think this move, aside being good for Briar's future, was good for many reasons," mom muses, giving me a knowing smile with one hand on her growing belly. "Also, Hunter was just talking about the annual camping trip coming up this weekend," she muses, looking at all of them. "Maybe you could take Briar this year."

No.

I swallow. Just what I need—alone, in the woods, with the four of them.

"I'm not really into camping—"

"Oh, come on," Ash pleads, gripping my knee tightly. "We have a big tent and an extra sleeping bag," he adds, his implication clear.

His hand slides from my knee up to my thigh to prove his point, but I brush it off and stand. "I need to get to school," I lie, grabbing my plate full of mostly uneaten food and heading to the kitchen. I feel someone behind me, and when I turn around, Samson is watching me with a frown. His arms are crossed, and he's leaning against the island. I'd almost forgotten he was here, too. He's always so quiet.

"You okay?" he asks, keeping his distance. "You hardly ate a thing."

"Yeah," I mumble, mimicking his stance and leaning against the sink. "I'm not that hungry. It's just…a lot. All of it. You guys, and Cam, and my mom, and Scarlett, and Jack…" I swallow, despite my constricting throat. "What if something happens to my mom? Or Hunter? Or Andrew?"

The thought has crossed my mind. If that night was any indication, Cam could be cruel and possessive, even though he knows how to hide it most of the time. And escaping prison just proved the fact that he has question-able morals. And now that my mom is pregnant…if he found out…

I'm worried something is going to swoop in and ruin this wonderful life we carved out for ourselves here—just when I'm beginning to call this place *home*.

Samson's jaw ticks as he takes a step toward me. "Cam is going to have to fight each of us to the death before he gets to you," he growls. "I should've talked to him when I saw him weeks ago," he adds with a hint of regret as he looks away. "I should've waited in my car, should've tried following him to see where he's staying..." He sighs, running a hand through his straight, dark brown hair.

"You were in shock," I answer, looking down at my boots. "I think we're all still in shock."

"We're going to find him, okay?"

I nod. "Okay."

Hopefully before he finds us.

A few minutes later, Hunter, Ash, and I climb into Hunter's car and head to school. We recently stopped driving separately, and they now wait for me every morning so that we can all drive together. It's sweet—and it makes me feel like a true part of their friend group. I smile as we pull up next to Ledger and Samson at school. Hopping out and throwing my backpack over my shoulder, I glance around quickly.

Everyone is watching us.

The attention I attract as one of *them* is startling. I don't really care about high school hierarchies or what any of the other students think. Knowing the Kings have my back makes the fact that Cam is wandering around Greythorn a little more tolerable, and it makes me feel... safe. Wanted. Cherished. As I walk in with them, I try to give everyone we pass a warm smile, but they all avert their eyes.

I'm not a monster, and neither are the Kings, but I understand now how reputations start—how rumors unfold.

It's unfortunate, but I vow to show everyone that there's nothing to fear.

꽃 4 꽃

BRIAR

I'm trying not to fall asleep in my pre-calculus class when there's a knock at the door. A younger guy walks up to the teacher, a stack of papers in his hand. Once he drops them off, the teacher distributes them to every desk, and my heart sinks when I look down at what it is.

Vote for homecoming King and Queen!

There's a space for nominating both King and Queen, and my pen hovers over the spaces. I can feel eyes on the back of my neck, and Scarlett and Jack are both watching me with wide eyes from a few seats up. They haven't spoken to me at all, so I'm not surprised when they begin whispering and looking away.

"Alright, guys," the teacher drawls. He's an older man in his fifties, balding, and extremely monotone. "Let's get back to learning."

I look down at the paper again. It's not due until next

Friday—and there's a drop box in the quad for people to insert their votes.

Someone laughs behind me. I turn around. A girl I don't know rolls her eyes.

"Don't think for a second that you or the Kings will win," she accuses snidely, gesturing to me. "It's usually one of the football players and his girlfriend. People actually *like* them."

My cheeks burn, but something fiery fills my chest. Some urge to prove to them that I'm not a monster, not someone to be feared or hated.

And neither are the guys—my *friends*.

Suddenly, I know what I have to do. Smiling, I fold my paper and put it in my backpack, and watch as others do the same. The dance is next Saturday—meaning I have exactly twelve days to get the entirety of the senior class to like me.

To like *us*.

They're going to vote for us, and we're going to win.

꧁❦꧂

At lunch, I sit with the guys in the middle of the quad. They've all purchased their gourmet lunch from the cafeteria, and I'm just about to go buy a sandwich and a cookie when Hunter sets a plate of food down for me.

"Eat," he commands.

I eye the delicious-looking, fire-roasted pizza that only a place like this would serve their students. "You bought me lunch?"

"Ash did," he murmurs.

I turn to face Ash. "Thank you."

"The line was really long." He shrugs. "I figured you wouldn't want to wait."

We eat as people make giant circles around us, ensuring they don't get too close. People aren't just scared of them—they *loathe* them. I know they've all done things to deserve that hate. To say they were completely innocent would be a lie, but I know now that these roles, these stereotypes they fall into were crafted without their consent. They fit the mold—the pigeonhole that someone, somewhere created.

It's so much easier to hate what you don't understand.

To outsiders, they're hard, unimpressed, cold. But I know them all to be warm, funny, and caring.

"I'm going to be homecoming queen," I state, smiling.

Samson clears his throat. "What do you mean? Don't you have to vote?"

I smirk. "Yes. But I'm on a mission to get people to like me." Hunter's lips twitch, and Ash and Ledger laugh. "What's so funny?" I ask.

Samson shakes his head. "Nothing. I just didn't think you'd care about something like that."

I shrug, looking around at everyone—everyone who is watching us, everyone with narrowed eyes and frowns on their faces. Everyone who hopes we *won't* win. People who are curious enough about us to attend the parties, whisper in the hallways... but would never admit to that curiosity.

"I don't. Not really. I just want to prove to everyone that you—that *we*—are not bad people. That maybe they might like us if they got to know us."

"Yeah, right," Ash huffs, biting into his sandwich.

"Not after Micah," Ledger adds, unsmiling.

"I don't think you get it," Hunter says slowly, frowning.

"I appreciate the optimism. I really do. But these people would rather burn us alive than appoint one of us as homecoming King." His eyes rove over my body, hesitating on my bare thighs for a split second. "And now that you're one of us..."

He doesn't have to say it. I'd been ignoring the fact that everyone now hated me since I parked next to them that day a few weeks ago. It's easier to ignore it—to pretend that I'm not detested simply by being with them. But I can't ignore the shifting gazes, the wide berths while walking, the whispers and murmurs.

"I'm going to do it," I say, my voice loud and clear. "Which one of you will be my King?"

Hunter's eyes narrow slightly, and Ash shifts uncomfortably in his seated position on the step. Ledger swallows. I look at Samson.

"Please?" I beg.

He sighs. "Fine."

"He's the nicest one," Ash mumbles. "It makes the most sense."

Samson gives Ash a soft look that I don't have time to decipher, and I take Samson's hand in mine.

"Thank you." Smiling satisfactorily, I drop his hand and take a bite of my lunch. "So, are we all going to the dance together?" I ask.

"Yeah, but we don't stay past the ceremony," Ledger adds, tilting his head. "We usually host a party at my house instead, since my parents are out of town on the weekends."

I don't know what to say to that. Out of all our parents, Andrew is the most normal, and Samson's parents are nice, yet busy. Ash's dad is...well...incapacitated, and his mother is still locked away in a psychiatric hospital. It's then that I realize I know nothing about Ledger's family, except that he comes from old money and is related to the famous author, and that his parents are very religious.

"What do they do?" I ask, taking another bite of the gooey pizza.

His eyes twinkle as he gives me a mischievous smile. "They're inspirational speakers."

I cup my mouth with my hand, trying not to laugh, but he nods.

"Oh, you're serious?"

"Very. They took my great uncle's fame and used it to their advantage. They're super religious and travel the country—sometimes the world—preaching about God and how most things are a sin."

I open and close my mouth. "I—wow."

He chuckles. "My older brother is a tattoo artist in Boston. And I'm...me. If that gives you any indication of how we turned out."

"Now the tattoos make complete sense."

He nods, chewing. "Yeah, they definitely didn't approve of those. Silas, my brother, started inking me when I was sixteen. At first, I did it to be rebellious, a big fuck-you to my zealot parents...but I actually really enjoy it now."

"His parents are nuts," Ash laughs, shoving Ledger's shoulder gently. "They won't even let me in the house."

I narrow my eyes. "Why?"

He winks at me and nudges his jaw toward Samson. "Both of us. Because we lie with men, and that's a sin."

My face falls. "Seriously? That's horrible."

"They're bigots," Ledger adds, "but we sure do have fun messing with them."

I laugh. "How so?"

Samson interjects. "I've had Out Magazine sent to the house for years. They keep canceling, but I keep sending it. Oh, and the hefty donations I've made in their name to various LGBTQ+ organizations. Imagine the horror when people find out New England's biggest bigots donate to the Human Rights Campaign and the Transgender Law Center." He smirks.

"That's amazing, and wickedly clever."

"Anyways, our homecoming party is always lit," Ledger muses.

Just as I'm about to ask about his brother, some freshman trips and falls, spilling his soda and spraying us. All four guys jump up, and Ash takes a menacing step forward.

"Watch where you're fucking going," he growls, and the kid scrambles up and runs away.

When he sits back down, I glare at him. "No wonder everyone's terrified of you guys," I say sharply. "If Samson and I are going to be King and Queen, you need to be nicer."

Hunter's jaw ticks as he watches me. "It's easier to keep them afraid of us. Other than you, we've only ever befriended one other person."

"You mean Micah?" I ask quietly.

The four of them go still. Hunter rubs his lips with his thumb and forefinger.

"Yes. With Micah. We decided then and there that we would continue the facade until graduation. Ash and Samson...if they weren't Kings... My father. Ash's father. Greythorn isn't as progressive as you might think. And Ledger's family..." He looks away, shaking his head. "If people weren't afraid of us, Briar, they would eat us alive. It happened once—one incident—and we almost lost our footing completely. It's just easier this way, like I said."

I look around—at the students who watch us, waiting —who look away the instant any of us make eye contact.

I swallow. "You're the most vulnerable, so you stay on the offensive," I murmur.

It all makes sense now.

Hunter nods. "None of us enjoy fucking with these kids," he starts, and then he looks at Ash. "Except maybe Ash," he jokes.

Ash punches him. "Shut the fuck up, man."

"Anyways, the point is, it kind of just happened after Micah, and we never questioned it. Yeah, maybe we play into it a bit. But we're just trying to survive. Like you. Like all of them."

I nod. "I get it. But I won't play along. I can't be an asshole just to hold up the silly status quo. And by this time next week, maybe we can change their minds about you. About *us*."

When I look at Samson, he's watching me with a mix of wariness and awe.

"I'll play nice," Ash concedes, standing.

"Me too," Ledger agrees from where he's seated.

Hunter cocks his head and gives me a lopsided smile. "Just tell me what to do, little lamb."

5

B<small>RIAR</small>

"No way," I mutter, glancing at the tent Ledger set up for us while I was helping Samson get dinner prepped.

"Oh, come on," he exclaims, throwing his hands out to the side. He looks like a tatted-up lumberjack in his flannel shirt and tan hiking boots. His blonde hair is haphazardly coiffed to one side, and his white teeth gleam in the late afternoon sun. "Don't knock it 'til you try it."

I twist my mouth to one side and cross my arms. "I don't sleep on the floor. Scientists and engineers invented beds for a reason."

He smirks and walks over to me. "How about we snuggle up together tonight? I'll make sure you're comfy..." He brushes his finger along my arm. I shiver at his touch.

"She gets her own room in the tent, dude," Hunter growls, walking past us. He's with Ash, and they have armfuls of wood.

"Did you just chop that?" I ask, impressed.

"You bet your ass we did," Ash replies, and I laugh.

"Okay, whatever. I don't care where I sleep, as long as I have some sort of cushion."

I walk off in search of Samson, ignoring whatever it is they're mumbling.

In hindsight, agreeing to an overnight camping trip with the guys was probably stupid. I mean, what did we expect would happen? My stomach clenches every time I think about what *could* happen—not just with one or two of them, but with *all* of them. There's no buffer here, no going home tonight, no hiding. We're here together, alone, out in the open. Whatever flame has been kindling between me and all of the guys is about to combust now that we're in a place like this together. I can feel it—the tension.

Nearly tripping over a large twig, I curse and cross my arms as I head toward the picnic tables. I don't hate camping, per se, but we just never went when I was growing up. My mom isn't exactly the rugged type. We took a lot of vacations to Disneyland and stayed in hotel rooms, and we went to Portland and Seattle a couple of times. Once, we went to Hawaii and sat by the pool for five days. To my thirteen-year-old self, that was the dream, and the extent of our vacationing.

But... I also needed this. The thought of getting away for a couple of nights sounded so appealing. Everything with Cam has been weighing on my shoulders, as well as getting everyone to like us before homecoming, Scarlett and Jack, my mom... I loved the idea of relaxing with all of them off the grid.

I swallow as I crunch through the foliage, spying

Samson at the grill. I tuck my hands into my puffy vest, and he smiles at me as I walk up.

"Getting hungry?" he asks. I clear my throat. "Very. I never knew that watching you all set up our camp from my place in the lounge chair would be so exhausting," I joke, cocking my head.

He laughs. "Yeah, well, someone has to do it."

Why is it so much easier to talk to him than any of the others? Maybe not Hunter, but Ash and Ledger, certainly. It's always so primal with them—physical, lusty, heady. With Samson, it feels like I'm dating my best friend most of the time.

Except for the night in his pool, when he most certainly was not a gentleman.

He turns the camping grill off, turning to face me. "I feel like we made a mistake bringing you up here," he murmurs, his eyes darkening ever so slightly behind his glasses. My pulse quickens as he scowls at me.

"What do you mean?" I ask, but I already know.

"Because it's wild here, and it brings out the wild in us," he starts, looking around. "There's no one around, and you're here with four guys who want to screw you every second of every day," he adds, laughing as he takes a step forward.

"I think you're exaggerating," I retort, rolling my eyes.

"Every second," he whispers, reaching up brush a strand of hair off my cheek.

"Let's eat!" Ash calls from behind me.

I spin around, and the other three guys come stomping over, and we begin our feast. Devouring my cheeseburger, I go back for seconds. I wasn't lying when I said lounging around while they set up camp was tiring. I could use a nap right about now.

The sun begins to set behind the pine trees, and the air cools significantly. Now I understand why Hunter packed extra blankets, hats, and gloves. It's the first week of October, and fall has begun in New England. In Greythorn, that means everything is Halloween themed all month long.

There's no one around.

Samson's words cause the hairs on my arms to stand on end.

They'd been here before—this was *their* spot, a place they came every year for the last four years. It wasn't a camping ground, but instead, an unrestricted area about an hour west, deep inside the dense forest. I don't even have cell service. I glare at my phone, sitting on the table with four others, useless in this damned place.

I get up and walk to Hunter's car, grabbing a blanket. When I get back, Ledger is stoking a fire.

"S'mores?" he asks, winking.

I look down longingly at the grocery bag at his feet filled with treats, but the forest is starting to get loud. I remember hearing that wild animals come out to prowl at dusk, and just then, a twig snaps in the distance.

"I think I'm going to go to bed," I whine, glancing in the direction of the noise.

"It's not even six," Ledger grumbles. "I thought we could play a game."

I blow out a loud breath of air. "There are critters out there, and I'd rather be safe in my tent when they arrive here to eat us."

Hunter hides his laugh behind his hand, but the other three guys burst out laughing.

I hate them all.

"Nothing is going to eat you," Ash chides, gesturing for me to approach. When I do, he pulls me down into his lap and moves my hair away from my ear, whispering, "Except me."

Goosebumps erupt on my skin as Ledger passes around the coat hangers and marshmallows. Ash is surprisingly calm underneath me, his hand on the flesh of my hip, but otherwise, he's distracted and talking to Hunter.

Once we've all gorged ourselves on S'mores, the campsite gets noisier with crickets chirping all around us. Ash pulls a blanket around us, and when I look up at the guys, they're all lit up from the fire.

"What about strip poker?" I suggest, and Hunter, Ledger, and Samson all look at me with dark, hooded eyes.

Hunter tilts his head, his hand propping his chin up as he leans back in his chair.

"Fuck, yeah."

❧ 6 ❧

BRIAR

Did I really just say that out loud?

Samson puts the fire out, and we all duck into the large, two-bedroom tent. I can't help but scold myself in my mind.

Way to sound desperate, Briar.

Someone must've placed a battery-powered lantern in here at some point because it's all lit up. There's one sleeping bag on a single air mattress in the smaller bedroom, and four sleeping bags are squished together in the other, larger room, which feels silly. I'm not exactly the virgin Mary.

We all sit in the large bedroom in a circle, leaving the opening unzipped a little for fresh air. Hunter walks to his backpack, pulling out a bottle of whiskey and a deck of cards. He passes the whiskey around, and we all take a sip. I cringe as it slides down my throat, burning. Wiping my mouth, I hand it to Samson on my left while Hunter holds the cards out.

"Okay, who knows how to play?" he asks.

"I do," I murmur. "Cam taught me." I look around, and Hunter is watching me with furrowed brows. Ash is sitting cross-legged, scowling. Ledger is playing with his tongue ring—something I wish he'd stop doing—and Samson is picking a piece of lint off his shoulder. "I guess he was good for one thing," I add, my stomach churning at the happy memory—now tainted with what Cam did to me.

"So, let's erase all memories of him then," Ledger offers, his voice low and deep. "Let's have some fucking fun tonight, because fuck him."

I swallow, looking between them all, and they all have determined expressions on their faces.

"Right. So for Texas Hold'em, we each get five cards," I say quickly, nodding to Hunter. He doles out our hands, and then I get into explaining the different types of hands —royal flush, straight flush, 4 of a kind, etc. "I think it'll be easiest if we play a straight five-card draw, so from our five cards, we can take turns exchanging one or more of them from the remaining deck." I look at Hunter, and then at each of the guys. "Ready?"

"Easy enough," Ash muses from across from me. "You start, little lamb."

This place brings out the wild in us.

I can feel all of them watching me, and the hairs on the back of my neck begin to tingle.

We take turns exchanging cards until we're all satisfied with our hands. We each lay down our cards. I have a straight flush, but Ledger has a royal flush.

"I win," he smirks, nodding to my jacket. "Strip."

33

My eyes snap to his, and something heated looks back at me. Something, not someone—almost like he's no longer human. Not my friend—but an animal. I pull my lower lip between my teeth as I remove my jacket, and Samson begins to reshuffle the cards for the next round.

"You guys have to strip, too," I command, glaring at Hunter, Ash, and Samson.

And they do.

The air turns then—and I'm suddenly so aware of that fact that all five of us are out here together. *Alone.* Teenage hormones raging, dirty thoughts racing...it's not like there's not a precedent. Aside from Ledger, I've slept with all of them. So why are my hands shaking? Don't I trust them? Is it just being with them together—or the uncertainty of what could happen? Up here, it almost feels like there are no rules.

We continue to play. I manage to win the next round, and as the guys take off another article of clothing, my senses awaken. I can smell the cologne Hunter uses, and the laundry detergent on Samson's shirt. The light, while bright, feels artificial, and I reach over to turn it down a couple of notches so that it's dimmer in here. I can feel the body heat radiating off each of them—and my own, as my chest flushes with color at Ash's lingering gaze. The clicking of the shuffling cards reverberates down my spine as Samson shuffles, his eyes never leaving mine. I end up losing my shirt, and then my pants, and I must actively keep my gaze on the floor of the tent, the plastic sticking to the backs of my bare thighs.

Hunter bought me a few new lingerie sets, including this one—a white, lace push-up bra that does wonders for my boobs, accompanied by a high-waisted, white thong.

"You wore *that* to camp?" Samson grits out, incredulous.

"I bought it for her," Hunter mumbles.

A twig snaps outside the tent, and the adrenaline that courses through me, the way my heart pounds against my ribs, just adds to the intensity of the game. The dim light exaggerates our shadows, so that each movement causes the light in the large tent to flicker. I swallow as the only sound I hear is an owl hooting, and the cards flicking against the fabric of the tent floor. Everyone is silent, and I dig my nails into my palms nervously. Each of them still watches me like a hawk—like they want to take turns devouring me whole.

I can't help but admit to myself that I want them to.

I want all of them.

Hunter and Ledger are down to underwear and socks. Samson is mostly clothed, and Ash has pants on. My eyes find his, and I swear I see something feral moving behind them.

This place brings out the wild in us.

By the time Hunter strips completely naked two rounds later, we've all had a few more sips of whiskey, and the air inside of here is stale, warm, and blistering with tension. My clit throbs, and my stomach keeps dipping with butterflies. I lose a bra, but I wrap my arms around myself.

Ledger gets naked next, and then Samson. I lose the next round, and I peel my thong off. I can hear Samson's shallow breathing from here. Ash concedes, and then he removes his pants.

I look down at the ground, unsure of what I'll find

when I look up. Four hungry beasts? Will they be nervous? Will it be gentle or rough? How does this work?

"Come here," Ash commands, leaning forward. I suck in a breath of air as his large erection stands up straight, the thick head already wet with pre-cum. His shaft is veiny, dark, and it intimidates me. "I said, come here."

"Ash—"

"Whenever we want you. However we want you," he reminds me, his eyes dark. "You took an oath. You're ours."

Hunter scowls and clears his throat. "Dude, she doesn't have—"

"I want to," I squeak, sitting up straighter. They all stare at me, and I crawl on my hands and knees over to Ash.

Kneeling next to him, I smile. "How do you want me?"

7

ASH

I reach out and grab Briar gently by the hair, pulling her onto my lap so that she's facing me. Groaning, I kiss her and use my other hand to play with her taut, pink nipple. She opens her mouth with every twist, and tiny moans come out of her throat. I thrust my heavy cock into her slit, sliding it in and out, not penetrating her yet but needing friction.

God, she smells like fucking vanilla. Always. I can't fucking get enough.

I pull away and see Hunter moving down her neck and placing a kiss on her shoulder. Samson slides one hand around my torso, and he kisses my earlobe.

I nearly explode.

It's a lot of heavy breathing, skin brushing against skin, the scent of whiskey permeating the air. Ledger moves to

Briar's other side, stroking his cock and rubbing it against her leg.

This is so fucking hot.

"Who wants her first?" I ask, smiling.

Her eyes widen, and I hope she knows I'm only half-joking.

"Let her pick," Hunter growls, staring at me.

"Ledger," she whispers, rubbing her pussy on my cock now. Her pupils are darkened, and her eyelids hooded. She climbs off me and gestures to him. "Lie down." Then she looks over at Hunter. "Get behind me."

She's nervous, but the two-word commands are purely her animalistic urges coming to light.

I'm fucking here for it.

I watch in what feels like slow motion as Ledger lies down, and she straddles him, his cock bouncing every time she brushes against it. Her pussy is gleaming. Hunter comes behind her and reaches around to her front, swirling his fingers against her clit. She bucks her hips and slides against Ledger, jerking him off with her pussy. He puts his hands over his face, and I notice his toes curling. Hunter's cock teases at her ass.

"Hey," Samson whispers, pulling me backwards onto his lap. I shudder. I forget how strong he is, how completely ruthless and powerful he is in bed. It's so different from the guy everyone knows him as—the guy in glasses who is smart as hell and the nicest one of us all.

"Do you have lube?" I whisper, grinding against him as I watch my three friends before us.

"In my backpack," Samson mutters. I crawl over and find it in the front pocket. My cock is wet with pre-cum as

I move back toward him, and I see Briar watching us with a mirthful smile.

Fuck yes.

I look back at Samson, on my knees before him as I cup his erection. God, I love his piercing. He groans, the sound reverberating through the air. His breath is ragged, and his throat bobs as he swallows.

"Bend over," I demand. He gets on his hands and knees, and I lube my shaft generously, tossing it to Hunter. Samson strokes his cock slowly with one hand as I press my head against his opening. Gently, I nudge myself into his ass, and he hisses.

"Fuck," he mutters, his voice frayed. "Fuck."

It's hot and *so, so* tight. He clenches against me, and I groan.

"You feel so fucking good," I mutter, looking over at Briar. She's bent over Ledger now, and he's pressing into her. Hunter is poised to fuck her ass next.

With every slow thrust into him, Samson lets out a sharp breath.

"Harder," he rasps. "I want to feel all of you."

His knuckles are white as he fists the sleeping bag underneath us. We both look over at Briar, who's mouth is open as she takes Hunter *and* Ledger in fully.

"Fuck," I whisper, my cock hardening even more at the sight of my friends, of Briar being filled just like she was with Samson and me a few weeks ago.

I let out a few sharp breaths and quicken my pace. Hunter's hands are gripping Briar's ass firmly as he pounds into her, and his face is contorted into something feral and needy. He's massaging her clit and she moves into his hand, throwing her head back so that her long hair is trailing nearly down to her ass. Ledger meets each of Hunter's thrusts so that they're diving into her rhythmically.

Underneath me, Samson quickens his pace as he jerks himself off, moaning and meeting me with every thrust. My balls tighten, and I feel my climax getting close. My head falls back as I cry out, upping my tempo and squeezing his ass cheek.

"I forget how good it feels when you fuck me," Samson growls, his hand moving quickly along his length. "So fucking good," he whispers.

"I'm going to come," I rasp, my whole body tensing as pulses of pleasure begin to coil, ready to release in a fountain of come.

"Fill me, baby," he answers, his voice hoarse. The way he says it sends me over the edge, and I spill into his ass, filling it with every pulse of my cock.

My breathing is ragged and heavy, and I'm still twitching several seconds later. When I look up at Briar, she's watching us with a darkened expression. She turns to Samson.

"I want you to come in me when these two are done."

❦ 8 ❦

BRIAR

I never knew something like this was even...possible. It's beyond what I'd ever imagined. My elbows sting from the coarse blankets as Hunter pounds into my ass from behind, and Ledger moves underneath me, their shafts filling me. Like the time with Ash and Samson, I feel *so* full, stretched to the brim, feeling like any wrong movement could tear me in half. With that pain though...comes immense pleasure. A pleasure so deep, so visceral, that my whole body craves it—my whole body responds to it.

Watching Ash and Samson together is the hottest thing I've ever witnessed. Sparks of pleasure course through me, my legs shaking as Hunter grunts from behind me. He slaps my ass, and I cry out.

"Harder," I groan, and he slaps my ass cheek again. This time, the pain lingers, and it intensifies how full I feel with both inside me.

Ledger circles his hips underneath me, his cock hitting the perfect spot inside me and his thumb pressing against my clit, having taken over for Hunter. I buck my hips, and everything everywhere feels like it's on fire. My body begins to quake, and something fiery hot and intense as fuck shoots through me. I feel a gush of liquid underneath me.

"Holy fuck, you're soaking me," Ledger mutters. His voice is broken, edged with something like disbelief and awe. "God, you're so fucking beautiful," he growls.

When I look down at him, his face is sweaty, his eyes vulnerable and open. I can't concentrate—I'm drifting between nearly unconscious and too conscious of what's happening. I'm no longer a person—just a body, just a large muscle waiting to unfurl.

I throw my head back and ride Ledger, gliding back and forth on top of him as Hunter meets my movements. I reach back for him, and he takes my hand, squeezing it firmly.

"Come for me," Ledger demands. "I want you to soak me again." His voice is serious, concentrated. He flicks my clit hard, and I nearly tell him to stop, but when he does it again, everything springs open, and I lose control of my body completely. Waves of undulating pleasure coarse through me, and I notice another gush of liquid as my hips buck uncontrollably. I can't speak, can't move, can't do anything until it's over. With my mouth open, I collapse on top of Ledger, gasping.

His hands cup my face as he continues to fuck me. "Has that ever happened to you before?"

I shake my head. "No. I didn't think it was possible."

"Do you want me to come inside of you?" he whispers, slowing down.

I nod. "Yes."

"I'm close," Hunter growls, slapping my ass again. "Let's come together."

And then they do. It's a mix of roaring, grunting, and throbbing—I can feel both turn to steel inside me as they empty themselves, and I sit up and watch as Ledger pulses to completion, groaning. Hunter pulls out first, and this time, I anticipate the strange feeling of that happening. Ledger pulls out next, and I fall onto my back, squeezing my legs together. I twist my face to Samson and give him a small smile.

"You next."

Who the hell am I with these guys? I feel like the confident, sexually awakened version of myself that I always hoped to be.

Samson strokes his hard cock and hovers over me. "That was so fucking hot," he murmurs, kissing my jaw. "But I want you to come with me."

Before I can stop him, he moves down and presses his face into my pussy.

"But—they—"

"It's fucking delicious," he says, licking slowly.

"Dude," Ledger says, his voice weak. "I'm straight, but that's fucking sexy as hell."

Hunter sits back and watches us, a small smile playing on his lips. "I don't know if I'm straight anymore knowing you're eating my come. I'm already hard again."

Samson chuckles, and I start to laugh, but then Samson's tongue darts into me, and he inserts two fingers, curving them so they hit my G-spot. I arch my back and cry out as his tongue slides hungrily up and down my slit, tasting me—*feasting on me.*

I feel like my body is levitating, like the pleasure is too much, and I'm ascending into the sky. It's a religious experience, and I don't know how I'll ever be able to go back to one sexual partner. Not after this—not after having three of them at the same time.

"Oh god," I whisper, my voice fraying. My legs begin to shake again, and Samson curves his fingers even more, hitting some unknown nerve that sends me skyrocketing into an orgasm and soaking his hand.

"Good little lamb," he murmurs. "At least we know you're not faking it."

My body is still jerking as he removes his fingers and slams his cock into me, and the fullness, the steely, hard warmth of having him inside me...

As my legs tremble, I grip onto his hair and wrap my legs around his torso. He sits up slightly and takes one leg, moving it over his shoulder. The angle—oh god, the angle. It clips the end of my orgasm but ensures another one immediately—something about his piercing, I think, because it feels like seven fingers at once as I spray everywhere.

"Good girl," he murmurs, slamming into me. "I'm coming."

He convulses on top of me, and I turn to look at the other guys. Hunter is jerking his cock quickly, breathing heavily, and he walks over to me on his knees, spraying my tits with come.

"Fuck," he groans, bucking his hips. "You drive me fucking wild," he rasps.

My eyes flutter closed, but a second later, I open them as Ash does the same, spilling on my torso.

"Briar," he moans, shaking. "Fuck."

I crane my neck to see Ledger stroking his shaft, and he crawls to me, giving me a cocky smile before throwing his head back and releasing on top of where Samson and I are still joined.

A wave of exhaustion slams into me, and I hear the guys muttering something about how they need to clean me up. A few seconds later, I feel a cool wipe cleaning me, from top to bottom, followed by a towel drying. Someone kisses my forehead, but I can barely keep my eyes open.

"Briar, you need to use the restroom." *Hunter.* "I'll take you."

It's an ordeal, but once I dress and pee, he brings us back to the tent. Handing me a face wipe, I shake my head. He *does* force me to drink water, and again, they murmur quietly to each other. Ash flicks the light off, and we shuffle into the large bedroom.

I feel Hunter climb in behind me, and Ash curls up on my other side.

"I knew you wouldn't need that extra sleeping bag," Ash whispers, stroking my face. "My beautiful, little lamb."

"Night, Briar," Hunter whispers in my ear. I can't see Samson or Ledger, but I know they're close by.

I fall asleep to Ash's hand grazing my jaw and Hunter's fingers caressing my back.

Yeah, I could get used to this.

9

SAMSON

I'm up before anyone else, and the light outside is still a soft pink. Yawning, I throw a hat and jacket on, finding my jeans in the corner of the tent—along with the empty whiskey bottle and pack of cards splayed out haphazardly.

Last night wasn't a surprise, and it certainly didn't feel wrong in any way. We all know Briar likes all of us, and we all like her. I mean, *fuck*, Ash and I had slept together before, so even that wasn't anything new. But the experience of being there with my friends, of somehow sharing that intimate moment... Most people might feel strange after a night like last night, but I feel euphoric. We were already close. This just brought us closer.

I walk through the woods and take a piss, and when I'm done, I find a small stream and sit on a rock, watching the water move over the smooth stones. I pick at the moss on the flat surface, and the soft, velvety feel reminds me of

Briar. A few weeks ago, she wasn't a part of our life at all, and now she's such a visceral part of our everyday existence.

It reminds me of something my parents told me once. There's a specific kind of gene in a person's body—babies, specifically, because they're constantly regenerating new cells—that stays dormant as they develop in the womb. That is, until something very specific happens—an event or incident, sometimes chalked up to something as minor as a mother's diet. When this gene comes alive, it can create a miracle...or cause devastation. Briar is the special gene in our group. Until her, we stayed dormant. But then she entered our lives, and it's like she changed our brain chemistry. The question is, will she create a miracle, or cause devastation?

A couple hours later, I walk back to the campsite, and this time, Ash is working the camping stove.

"Morning," he grumbles, handing me some instant coffee.

"Morning," I reply. "Thanks for the coffee."

"It's the least I could do," he mutters, smirking. "I should probably buy you dinner first next time."

I laugh. Ash confounds me sometimes. On the one hand, he's very supportive of the fact that I'm bi, and he's confessed a couple of times while drinking that he knows he's bi, too. But his upbringing really fucked him up because he's almost ashamed to admit it out loud. Like that would make it real, instead of keeping everything behind closed doors. I know he thinks it'll ruin his reputation at Ravenwood.

"Nah. You're good. I love coffee more than food."

Something passes over his face, and he gives me a small

smile. I see it then—the validation he always seems to need.

"Last night was phenomenal," I add, holding my cup out.

He clinks his cup against mine. "Yeah, she was pretty hot."

I tilt my head. "I'm not just talking about Briar."

He looks away and swallows. "Yeah man. Hey, do you want to help me with breakfast?"

When he looks at me again, he's almost pleading. *He's not ready, and that's okay.* He'll admit it out loud—he'll come out—when he's ready.

And I'll support him every step of the way.

"I'd love to."

10

BRIAR

Everything hurts.

Whoever said sex isn't a workout obviously never had a gang bang with four guys.

I laugh to myself as I pull my clothes on, grabbing my boots, my jacket, and a hat before unzipping the tent. The air is so much cooler out here than it is in Greythorn, and I shiver as I make my way to where everyone is gathered, the smell of bacon and eggs cooking on the camping stove wafting through the air. I'm the last one to wake up, rightfully so, and when I sit down at the picnic table, I expect all the guys to go quiet, or to get awkward, but they don't.

Hunter hands me a cup of coffee, and Ledger sits next to me, handing me a banana.

"Eat," he commands, raising his eyebrows.

"Yes, father," I joke.

His eyes darken ever so slightly. "Don't say shit like

that," he grumbles, leaning forward. "That kink could get very out of control for me."

I nearly choke on my coffee. "Good to know," I retort, chuckling.

And then it's business as usual—the same sort of camaraderie we normally have together. Joking, laughing, flirting...

As we eat our delicious breakfast—and by eat, I mean scarf like I haven't eaten in years—I look around at each of them.

I'm starting to fall for all of them in different ways, each having their own relationship and story with me. I swallow, suddenly *so* full. How will this all play out? I'm really beginning to care for them. Will I just continue dating all of them together? Will they eventually get jealous? What happens if we break up—one of us, or all of us? I'm reminded of Scarlett's words a few weeks ago on the phone.

You really think they won't fight to the death for you?

I wipe my hands on my jeans and sit back, studying each of them. Remembering last night, how my body—and now my heart—wants all of them equally. But there's four of them, and only one of me. I couldn't ever possibly choose.

Will they eventually *make* me choose? If things were to get serious with one or more of them? When it's no longer just about hot sex and fun?

I get ready for the day, using the makeshift shower Hunter rigged up on a tree. The water is ice cold, but at least I feel clean afterwards—especially after last night. I throw my damp hair into a ponytail and pull on leggings, a wool sweater, and a jacket. The weather really took a turn last night, switching to autumn officially. My nose is numb as I pull on my hiking boots. I'm shaking as I walk up to the fire, and warming my hands next to the hot flames is a welcome reprieve.

"Jeez, it's cold," I mutter, my teeth chattering. The guys are already in jackets and boots, forgoing a shower since we don't have much water. They're all sitting in camping chairs.

"You're *so* from California," Samson teases.

"Do you even know what snow is?" Ledger adds, leaning back and smirking.

I swat the back of his head. "Shut up."

"We have more jackets in the car," Hunter offers. "If you're cold."

I shake my head. "No. I think I'll be fine." My voice isn't as convincing as I would like, so I change the subject. "What are we doing today?" Yesterday was spent driving up here and setting up camp, and it's only nine, so I know we have all day for adventuring.

The guys all share a look, and I swallow. "Do I even want to know?"

Hunter laughs. "So, there are these caves," he starts, looking at his friends. "Supposedly, it's where the Boston Baptist got started."

I look among all of them, racking my brain. "Who?"

Ledger snorts, but it sort of sounds like *oh, boy.* I narrow my eyes at Ash, who is looking away.

"Who is the Boston Baptist?" I hiss, my hands on my hips.

"A crazy, religious zealot," Ledger chimes in. "It's who inspired my parents to become the monsters they are today."

My lips thin. "And why would we go to his cave?"

Hunter's lopsided smile widens. "Because it's sick as fuck. And there's something we've always wanted to do there."

"Something? Your version of *something* is setting fires and vandalizing buildings."

"And? You in?" Ash asks, leaning forward in his folding chair.

I cross my arms. "Do I have a choice?"

A few minutes later, we're trekking through the wilderness, a backpack of food and water at the ready on each of our backs, as well as baby wipes if anyone needs the restroom. I start to warm up as the sun begins to poke through the tall pine trees. I tie my jacket around my waist and pocket my hat, and about an hour later, we come to the side of a small hill. Sure enough, there are rock formations and an entrance to what I can only assume is the cave.

"You guys have a depraved adventurous streak," I add, panting. None of them look like they even broke a sweat, but I am damp and breathing heavily just from walking. "The house in the hills, and then Medford Asylum—"

"It's not a depraved adventurous streak," Samson interrupts, his voice ripe with warning. I glance at Hunter, but he's looking away. Ash, too—they both have haunted looks on their faces. "The house in the woods is where they found Charlotte Ravenwood's body," he murmurs. "And Medford is...well...it was a giant 'fuck you' to Christopher Greythorn."

I swallow as I look between Ash and Hunter. "I'm sorry. I didn't mean—"

"We had a bucket list of things we wanted to do our

senior year. Knowing that we could probably get away with most of it, we followed through. All of us have a past that haunts us, Briar. Even you." Samson just shakes his head, and I shift my weight from one hip to the other. "If you had an opportunity to get revenge, wouldn't you?"

They all take a step toward me, and I suddenly feel like an animal being hunted.

"Isn't that what we're doing with Cam?" I ask, my voice weak.

"Why do you think we wanted to help you?" Hunter muses, his brows furrowed. "This is our year, Briar. Our year to set things right. We don't want to go off to college —or wherever the fuck we decide to go next fall—and wonder if we did enough. We have an agenda." He looks back at the cave. "The question is, are you in?"

I look at the cave, and then at each of their faces. I have no idea what the cave represents, but knowing them, they have a reason for being here.

They're helping me.

The least I can do is return the favor.

"I'm in," I retort, scowling. "I thought the blood oath was a good indication of that." I walk past all of them and into the cave first.

I don't look back to see if they're following, because I know they are.

11

LEDGER

I shift my backpack and adjust the straps as we weave through the cavern. It's fucking cold in here without the strong sun beating down on us.

Briar pulls her jacket on. "Where are we headed?" she asks, looking around.

I swing my backpack around and hand everyone a flashlight. "Straight until it forks, then go left."

I hadn't spent months researching the Boston Baptist and the layout down here for nothing. We're all quiet as we head deeper into the cave. It becomes less of a bear cave, and more of an underground, natural-wonders type cave the farther we get and the lower we descend. I once read these caves snake through the underground of most of Western Massachusetts. No one has mapped the entire thing yet. It's just too large. I ignore the cold sweat along my brow when I think of accidentally getting lost down here.

When we get to the fork, I stop and set the backpack down. Briar sits on a large rock and winces, still sore from last night. I can't help but smile as she rolls her eyes at me. I've had my fair share of experimental sexual encounters, including three and foursomes, but last night was incredible. I swear Briar blushes as she looks away.

My little lamb.

"So, are we just waiting to get murdered, or..." she trails off and looks around. "This place is creepy."

The cave is still low and narrow here, but I see an open cavern filled with a natural spring up ahead. That's where Samuel Kent, also known as the Boston Baptist, used to hang out with his followers. He had quite a few. I know because my parents were two of them.

I start pulling supplies out of the backpack, and Briar's eyes find mine as I get the Micro-Blaster set up.

"What's that?" she asks skeptically.

I smirk. "It's called a Micro-Blaster. Uses blank cartridges and black powder to blast through rocks and other hard things—safely." I look around. "I wanted to get dynamite, but no one sells it anymore, and I didn't want us caved in from the blast."

Ash takes a swig of water. "Pussy," he mutters, and we all laugh.

Hunter points to a spot on the wall. "See that?" he asks Briar, taking a step back. "That's the rock he used as an altar. They thought Jesus would descend from the sky to this very cave," he adds, practically growling. "This wall—this rock— was mecca." He looks at the wall with repugnance. "It's been worn down with time, but it's still a place of worship for some crazy ass people." The surface is smooth, almost like a large painting, smeared with age and dirt and minerals.

She's breathing heavily as she looks among all of us. "So, what? We're going to blast it with that thing?" She looks at me with wide eyes.

Samson swings his backpack off his back. "Would being caved in with the four of us really be so bad?" he jokes, pulling a drill out of his backpack and beginning to drill the holes into the surface of the rock.

She doesn't seem to find his joke funny, because she frowns and leans forward in her seated position. "I swear to god," she mutters. "You guys are fucking nuts."

"We didn't get our reputation for nothing," I chide, smiling. I hand Hunter the detonating device. "Back up," I warn, looking down at her. She scrambles up and takes a few steps back. "It's just going to crack down the middle. And then we're hauling the rock into the spring."

She shakes her head, and Hunter nods once as we all back up several feet. The explosion isn't as loud as I thought it would be, but the entire face of the rock falls off, as if some invisible force cracked it straight down the middle. The four of us squat down to pick it up, and we hurl it into the spring a few feet away. The splash is satisfying, and when we get back, I smile.

The face of the rock is gone—in its place is a jagged, inverted wall.

We leave a few minutes later. I grab Briar's hand and pull her behind me since it's dark in here. When we get outside, she turns around to face us.

"Well, that was sort of anticlimactic," she jokes. "The fire and the spray paint were like...exhilarating, and—"

"Samuel Kent molested my brother," I interrupt. I don't mean to be rude or angry, but it's something she should know. "When we were younger, before my parents' cut ties with Samuel, he was over one evening and stayed the night. Silas was ten. I was four. I barely remember it, and to my parents' credit, they severed ties with him immediately. It doesn't absolve them of their craziness, but they did do that one thing right."

She goes completely still. Her mouth falls open and her eyes widen. "Ledger, I—"

"Not everything has to be a big production," I add, crossing my arms. "Sometimes the smallest actions can have the biggest consequences. While today might've been more satisfying with dynamite or caving the whole fucking place in, what we did will have a ripple effect. Think of doing something like that to the Western Wall. It may seem like a small infarction, but the altar is tarnished now. It's not inaccessible. It's tainted. And quite frankly, I think that's worse."

Briar looks between Hunter and me, and Hunter takes a step toward her. "Those fuckers deserve what we did. For what they did to Silas."

She shifts uncomfortably. "I get it, trust me. I want the same for Cam."

"Exactly," Samson muses, placing his hands in his pockets. "Like I said earlier... if you had an opportunity to get revenge, wouldn't you?"

12

BRIAR

Luckily, the rest of the afternoon isn't nearly as heavy as the caves. We fish in the nearby lake, catching a large trout to eat for dinner, and then we drink beer and play another round of war—except this time, we keep our clothes on. When it's time to cook dinner, Hunter grills the fish and Samson cuts some potatoes and carrots, and we all drink a little too much, indulging in a little too much food, too much beer, too much...everything. By the time I inhale my S'more, I'm ready for sleep. Being in nature is exhausting.

I head to bed alone, and tonight, there don't seem to be any shenanigans—yet. I undress and climb into one of the sleeping bags, and just as I pull it up to my chin, Samson unzips the tent and begins to undress. Without a word, he crawls in behind me, clad only in his boxers. He takes his glasses off and snuggles up against my back. It feels so good. I'm so cold that my body is shaking. His hand slides against my stomach, the warmth spreading through my core, as his chest presses against my back.

"You're freezing," he murmurs, tugging me closer. I feel his legs wrap around mine, and I stop shivering instantly, his warmth seeping into me. I run my finger along his forearm, and he shudders. "Go to sleep, Briar," he growls.

I don't obey—obviously. Especially not when I feel his hard length against my ass. Heat floods me, and I arch my back into him slightly as he hisses.

"I said, go to sleep," he chides, but there's amusement in his voice.

"I can't with that thing poking me."

He chuckles, the sound low and deep. It reverberates through me.

"I can't help but remember how good it felt to be inside of you," he mutters, sliding his hand underneath my bra, his thumb and forefinger gently twisting my peaked nipple.

"Fuck," I whisper, grinding my ass against him.

"Stop doing that unless you want me to fuck you," he growls.

I stiffen. "Then fuck me." Before he can move, I climb on top of him, throwing the sleeping bag off and trying not to balk at the cold. He pulls his boxers down, a low sound in his throat as he does. I don't even ask before I move my underwear to the side and sit on his hard shaft, slowly letting his thick head press against my opening until he slides into the hilt. *Holy shit.* His piercing really does enhance everything.

"Why do you feel so fucking good?" he groans, watching us as I move up and then down again, slamming against him—hard. Slowly. He moans. "God, I just fucked you, and I already feel like I'm about to explode."

I whimper as I drive down on him again, the sound of our joining permeating the air. My nipples are hard and sensitive from the cold, which only enhances the feel of his large cock inside me. Throwing my head back, I move my hips back and forth, but then he stops me.

"Let me," he rasps, and before I can protest, he flips me onto my back in one swift movement, slamming into me.

"Oh, god," I cry as he moves both of my legs over his shoulder. He's so impossibly deep now—I can feel it nearly at my belly button as he drives into me.

A finger comes around and works my clit, using my wetness as lube. Feverishly, he swirls two fingers against me, *almost* too rough, but the calloused skin is exquisite. I cry out as he changes his angle slightly, leaning back, and that's when I nearly lose it underneath him.

"You like that?" he murmurs, his tongue in his cheek. When I look up at him, his hair is in front of his face, and his expression is wild.

Samson Hall has come undone.

"Your piercing," I gasp, my voice uneven. "It...it..." I lose my train of thought as my eyes squeeze shut. My body tightens with every stroke of his fingers, every thrust of his cock, waiting to release like a spring that's been coiled for far too long.

"Look at us," he commands, dropping my legs and looking at where we're joined. I wrap them around his body and look down, his cock gleaming as he slowly slides in and out. "Look at us," he repeats, his voice breaking on the last word. I clench around him, the first wave of my climax tipping me over the edge. "Briar," he rasps, stilling as his shaft hardens even more.

And then he roars, sending me spiraling. I moan as he pulses into me, and I honestly don't care if the guys hear us, or if a bear eats us. Right now, all I care about is the fact that I am soaking Samson, and he's baring his teeth as his body shudders on top of me. My release slides down my spine, so potent that I know the sleeping bag is going to be soaked.

"Fuck," he whispers, collapsing on top of me.

I cover my face and laugh. "I came in here to sleep."

He chuckles, lying down next to me. "Then let's clean up and go to sleep."

A few minutes later, he's back in his position behind me. My body is heavy, and I feel so...content. Safe. Warm.

"Goodnight, Briar," Samson whispers in my ear.

I drift off before I can even reply.

13

BRIAR

The next morning, we eat a quick breakfast before packing up camp and heading out. This time around, I actively try to help break down the tent and load the car, and Hunter laughs as he watches me try to fold the tent poles so that they fit in the bag. He eventually takes them from me and packs everything up seamlessly.

It was an honorable attempt on my part.

We took two cars here, and since I rode with Ash and Ledger on the way up, I decide to ride with Hunter on the way home. Samson decides to catch a ride with the others, seeing as they're all going back to his house. Before we start our drive, Hunter turns on his playlist, and I sit back against the luxurious leather as he drives us toward home.

"Camping isn't *so* bad," I muse, twirling my hair as I look out at the two-lane road ahead. Tall pine trees surround us, like the ones in town—except here, in true nature, they're about three times taller.

He chuckles. "I told you. I knew you'd enjoy it."

I look away so that he doesn't see me blush.

"We've been going every year since my mom died," he adds, rubbing his jaw.

I play with the hem of my sweater. "When did she..."

"Freshman year. I was fifteen." I wait for him to continue, but he just clenches his jaw and looks straight ahead.

"We don't have to talk about it," I say, my voice soft.

He shrugs. "It still hurts. All these years later. It still feels like someone's jamming a knife into me whenever someone says her name."

I swallow. "Then let's change the sub—"

"But I feel like if I don't talk about her, that I'll forget all the nuanced things about her, you know?"

I nod. "I know."

He sighs and shakes his head, the indie music playing softly in the background.

"She was murdered intentionally. Because of who she was. Because of who her family was."

"The Brahmins?" I ask, remembering our conversation all those weeks ago.

He nods. "That was her maiden name. The authorities tracked her murderer down—he was a nobody, just someone obsessed with her. He's in jail now, and they traced two more bodies to him, so in a way, her death brought those two women to justice, too."

I'm quiet as I take in the information. "I'm so sorry, Hunter."

"He dumped her body right in front of that house. The one you caught us burning."

I nod. Nothing ever came of that, despite my worry that the fire would jump. I saw a small article on Twitter calling it an act of arson, but it didn't go any further than that. Ash was right that night. They'd taken precautions, and the fire remained contained to the house.

If you had an opportunity to get revenge, wouldn't you?

"Anyways, search dogs found her a day after she went missing. He'd..." He inhales sharply. "He'd *butchered* her, Briar. She was unrecognizable."

I grip the edge of the arm rest. "You saw her?"

He nods. "I was out there looking for her. So was my dad. I didn't expect..."

God.

At fifteen. Seeing your mother's mangled body at fifteen. What did that do to his mental health? How has that affected him?

"She was my best friend. The kindest, most genuine person. Happy—like all the time." He laughs, and I can tell it helps to talk about her. "Aubrey reminds me of her, actually. So do you."

I bark out a laugh. "I'm certainly not *happy* all the time. But thank you."

He smiles. "I just mean, people want to be around you. I know you think you're so different from your mom, but you both have this energy that puts people at ease."

I look down, my throat constricting. My entire life, I always felt like the runt. My mom is a goddess in every way possible. A Pinterest mom through and through, who goes to bed early and gets up at five in the morning to exercise. Who makes healthy smoothies for breakfast.

Who gets all her work done before two, so that she can volunteer in the NICU two afternoons a week. She has her shit together. On top of it all, I've always felt loved. *And* she became a mother so young... I am constantly in awe of her.

It's nice to know that perhaps other people see a little bit of her in me.

"Thank you for saying that."

"I think that's why my dad was drawn to her. And why I was drawn to you."

I swallow. "Your poor dad, too," I add, thinking of Andrew and what happened to his first wife.

"He took it pretty hard. We both did. I don't think we left the house for a month. But...then we did. And somehow, our relationship got better. We started traveling, and he encouraged me to see a psychiatrist, who helped with my depression."

That explains the Lexapro in his bathroom and the postcards on his wall.

"I'm glad you had each other," I mutter, looking at him. "I know the therapy life all too well. I'm glad he got you help."

He smiles, his wavy hair falling in his face before he brushes it back.

"Yeah. My dad is cool. He's pretty strict, despite what the other students think, and he rides my ass over the important things."

I smile. "I'm sure you give him a run for his money."

He laughs, shrugging. "I don't actually know if he knows exactly what me and the guys get up to. He says he does, but if he knew, he probably wouldn't let me leave the house."

I giggle. "He must have some sort of idea. Or perhaps he just picks his battles."

"What about you?" He turns to face me for a second. "Your father?"

I frown. "I don't know. When my mom told him she was pregnant their senior year of high school, he basically ghosted her. She never saw him again. But I do know he was a football player, and he went on to play for some college team in North Carolina," I add, shrugging. "Honestly, I'm glad I never knew him. My mom and I had an incredible relationship, and I'm not sure we would have had that if he were in the picture."

"What a piece of shit," he mumbles, brushing his lip with his finger. "To get a woman pregnant, and then not have the courage to stick around?"

I look down. "Yeah, I mean, I guess he was scared—"

"Bullshit. Every father-to-be is scared, Briar. You both deserved better."

His words eat at me, and my eyes start watering. The way he always stands up for me—how he always defends me and ensures that I know my worth...

I reach over and take his hand. "Thank you."

We're quiet most of the way back to Greythorn. I don't notice anything is amiss until I glance at Hunter, and he's scowling into the rearview mirror.

"What's wrong?" I ask, looking behind us. There's a black SUV behind us.

He shakes his head. "I don't know... I swear this guy is following me."

Chills erupt on my body, and the hair behind my neck tingles. Glancing back again, I realize with dread that the glare from the sun prohibits me from seeing the driver.

"Turn left," I instruct, pointing to a residential street just outside the main square. I twist around, my heart sinking as the black car follows.

My pulse quickens. "Again." I point to the street coming up.

Sure enough, as soon as we turn, the black car follows.

Panic floods through me. Hunter reaches for my hand. "Hey. It's probably just a coincidence."

I swallow. "No. It could be—"

Hunter lets out a breathy laugh. "No. This car has been following us since we left the road of the campsite. How the hell would Cam know we were there?"

I look behind us as Hunter continues to drive. "Okay, I read once that if this happens, keep driving and then pull into a police station."

Hunter nods. "Yeah, that makes sense." He turns right, weaving through the neighborhood quickly, barely stopping at the stop sign. I look behind us.

"Briar. don't worry. I'll get us to the station."

I wipe my palms on my pants, my heart thundering against my ribs. My feet bounce nervously as Hunter pulls into the parking lot of the Greythorn Police Station.

We both look behind us as the black car slows and then stops completely.

"Oh my god," I whisper, ducking.

Suddenly, it speeds off, plowing through a stop sign and barely missing a guy jogging in the crosswalk.

"It was just some stupid idiot," Hunter says quietly.

"He stopped—" I shake my head. "There were no license plates—"

"Briar," he purrs, taking my hand. "It's okay. We're okay."

"What if it was Cam?" I ask, my voice strained.

Hunter frowns, reversing until we're back on the main road. "If it was Cam, there's nothing we can do other than keep an eye out for black SUVs."

I nod. "Yeah."

We head home in silence, and I make the excuse of having to unpack as I walk upstairs alone. Mom and Andrew are out, but I know they'll be back soon. I bite my lower lip as I pace around my room. Was he following us? Did he—did he see us the first night?

The thought slams through me.

The tent—we left it open that night, exposed to the darkness—

No.

I'm just being paranoid.

Don't be stupid, pretty girl.

Cam's words from that night nearly ten months ago cause goosebumps to erupt on my skin, and I stalk to my dresser, pulling out the only pieces of athletic clothing I own. I have to get out—I have to move—I feel like I'm going to crawl out of my skin here. I pull on the leggings and matching top. After slipping into running shoes I've never worn, I pull my hair up and grab my phone. This is laughable—but I need to do *something.* I can't imagine just sitting around and going over the way the car slowed, the way it sped off a few seconds later...

I take a quick jog around the perimeter of the park, keeping to public places in the broad daylight. The sweat sticks to my chest and back, my hair stuck to the back of my neck. It's hard, but it feels—*good.* My phone says I ran a little over a mile, and I'm happy with that. *Progress.*

I am considerably happier and lighter at dinner with

my mom, Andrew, and Hunter. He must notice my improved disposition, because he keeps looking at me with a sidewards glance, as if trying to figure out what's different.

And the best part is, after collapsing into bed with pure, utter exhaustion, I don't have a single nightmare that night.

❧ 14 ❧

HUNTER

I slap my mid-semester report card on my dad's desk, smiling. "Happy?" I tease, gesturing to the line of A's.

He laughs, picking the slip of paper up and studying it. "Very nice, Hunter. I'm proud of you." I'm about to make some smartass retort when he continues. "I think having Aubrey and Briar here is helping, don't you?"

He doesn't have to say it—I know exactly what he means. The dynamic in our house was very masculine for so long. Thank God for house cleaners and personal chefs —we didn't know how to do a damn thing around here. It wasn't for lack of trying—it just felt different after my mom passed. I didn't realize until recently that it's nice having someone to make you smoothies, or check on you, or organize your sock drawer...

Or to fool around with in the basement.

"Yeah, I think it is."

He leans back in his black, leather chair, putting his hands behind his head. "And you and Briar seem to be getting along *very* well," he adds, his eyes flitting up to mine.

I swallow. "She's a nice girl."

Nice?

He watches me for a second too long, his eyes narrowing slightly. If he suspects anything is going on, he doesn't say it out loud.

Sighing, he nods. "I agree," he says slowly, smiling up at me. "Well, I'm very proud of you, son. I think we can agree that Jefferson High School is now officially off the table."

An excited thrill goes through me. I would've been fine there—I would've survived. But I'm really glad I won't have to leave Briar.

"Thanks, Dad. And about the *New Yorker*," I start, running a hand through my hair. "I think I want to apply to some creative writing programs in New York. Maybe a smaller liberal arts school or something."

I brace myself for his answer. We'd never really talked about my future at college. It was always just something I was definitely going to do. He went to Yale, and my mother went to Harvard, so I think he just assumed I'd pick an ivy league and go there.

Leaning forward, he looks up at me, a twinkle in his eyes. "I think you should do whatever the hell makes you the happiest, Hunter."

I swallow the lump in my throat as he stands, coming around the other side of the desk. He gives me a tight embrace.

For the first time since my mom died, it truly feels like

we're going to be okay.

❧ 15 ❧

BRIAR

I sit in front of my computer and fix my hair, waiting for Sonya, my therapist in California, to log on to our video session. We'd agreed on today a long time ago—a month after moving—thinking it would be ideal to settle in first before continuing our sessions. I'm excited to update her on everything.

The screen flickers, and Sonya smiles—looking perfect, as always. Dark ringlets, deep set eyes, full lips—she is beautiful.

"Briar," she smiles. "It's so good to see your face."

I wave at the camera. "Hi!"

"You look really good," she offers, tilting her head. "Your hair is different."

I shrug. "I have my bangs pinned back so I can run later."

Her brown eyes widen. "I didn't know you were a runner!"

I laugh. "I'm not. I actually hate it. But it really helps with...you know..."

The great thing about Sonya is that she knows what happened, but she never, ever brings it up. She always lets me introduce my trauma. Some weeks we don't even talk about it, and I think it's that camaraderie that allows me to trust her—to open up to her.

"I heard about what happened," she says glumly, referring to Cam escaping prison. "You seem to be handling it okay..."

I nod once. "Yeah, I'm trying."

"And your stepbrother is helping you feel safe?"

I swallow. "Yeah. I know it's wrong, but—"

"Briar," she interrupts. "Why do you feel like your relationship with Hunter is wrong?"

She knows everything—maybe not the explicit details, but she knows I'm sort of dating all four of them. That they've vowed to protect me.

"I don't know. Maybe because I don't want to disappoint my mom?"

It slips out before I can even process it. Sonya's lips thin. "I understand that, but don't you think she'd be delighted to know her daughter has found a group of men who not only respect her, but act as her guardian angels, in a sense?"

"I just don't want her to think our relationship will ruin the family dynamic if it doesn't work out. She already has so much on her plate—"

"Stop. Listen to what you're saying. *Her* plate. *Hers*. What about your plate? What if she doesn't care that her plate is full? What if that's just your assumption? Focus on *your* plate. Focus on balancing your life. That balance will seep into other aspects of your life, and your mother will notice. And I promise, all mothers just want to see their children happy."

I look down, my eyes stinging with tears. "You're right."

"Now, tell me about these guys."

I laugh, and once I fill her in about the camping trip—in which I leave out the gang bang—she places her hands together.

"I already see a difference in you, Briar. I think as long as you feel safe—as long as you implement our rules—evaluate your surroundings, listen to your gut, apply common sense—you will be okay. Love like this doesn't come to those who wait around. It comes to those brave enough to go after it."

"Love?" I ask, smiling.

"Briar, I hate to break it to you, but—"

Holding a hand up, I shake my head. "I like being with them. But it's not love. Not yet, anyway."

"I see. And your friends? The ones who are mad at you?"

I swallow. "They're still mad."

She softens her expression. "I think they'll come around soon. Just be honest with them."

We chat for another thirty minutes, and I update her on mom's pregnancy, the Homecoming Queen shenanigans, and everything else—but I leave out that Samson had run into Cam. I have a feeling she'd be obligated to notify the authorities, and I don't want to do that yet.

Saying goodbye, we schedule a session for every other

week until things calm down, and I sign off the video call. I head downstairs and grab some chocolate, and to my delight, Hunter is in the basement watching some travel show. I plop down next to him, handing him a piece. He just smirks.

I focus on the show, realizing with excitement that it's about Paris.

"Have you ever been?" I ask, hoping I don't sound too desperate.

He nods. "Twice."

I perk up and twist to face him. "And? Did you love it? Did you eat croissants and drink cappuccinos, and walk along the Seine? *Je voudrais me promener le long de la rivière avec toi*," I add, and his eyebrows shoot up as he smiles.

God, I love the way his smile lights up his face.

"I knew you could speak French, but I didn't know you could speak it so well. What did you say?"

I tilt my head and pop a piece of chocolate into my mouth. "It roughly translates to; I would like to stroll along the river with you."

He tugs me onto his lap, brushing a piece of hair off my face. "Briar, why do you think I'm watching this show?"

I shake my head, confused. "Because you're obsessed with berets and baroque architecture?"

A smile plays at his lips. "So that when I come visit you, we can stroll along the river together," he whispers, running a finger down my jaw, sending sparks and excited shivers down my spine.

Love like this doesn't come to those who wait around. It comes to those brave enough to go after it.

16

ASH

My shoes bounce against the linoleum as I sit at the table in the visitor's room. I cross my arms and chew on the inside of my cheek. *This is so fucked.* Glancing around nervously, I look at everyone else here waiting to see a family member or friend. Are they as nervous as me?

I'm about to see my mother for the first time in five years.

When I got the call this morning, I was unsure of how it was even possible. For five years, we've had phone calls here and there, but never in-person visits. I couldn't do it —couldn't bring myself to be here. Of course my father never pushed it. He'd gotten his way, and she was here against her will.

Involuntary commitment—that's what everyone called it.

It's been five years—five years since I've seen her golden skin, dark hair, light blue eyes...

Swallowing, I lean forward and run my hands through my hair.

Now she's waiting to be released.

Released.

They say it could be as soon as this week.

And of course there will be an investigation.

My father is in custody, and he went on record saying he wrongfully committed her, called for her release, and the doctors agreed. Two doctors were incriminated for going along with it, as well. He'd paid them off, obviously. No reputable doctor would've kept her here this long. It's completely outrageous. It wouldn't have been ethical, or legal. It just goes to show the stronghold he has over this city.

At thirteen, it wasn't the first time I'd seen my dad, the mayor, exercise his power, his family name. But it was the last time I stood on his side. For five years, it has been a battle of the wills—of me standing up for myself in exchange for a black eye.

Once, a broken arm.

I always wonder if people knew, or if they honest to God had no idea what he did to me—to us. I have to believe it's the latter. I can't fathom the idea of people looking the other way, but then again, Greythorn isn't exactly the mecca of honest, decent people. Luckily, the recent vandalization of Medford Asylum seemed to have gotten enough attention that everything is coming to light now—that enough people are beginning to ask questions, place calls, write articles...

My dad's confession cemented it.

And even though it tore me up inside to get here, even though I'm not sure what kind of person will be waiting for me, I'm here.

I don't think I've ever been this nervous about anything.

The main door swings open, and a guard lets a woman through.

A woman—my *mother*.

Some kind of warmth washes over me at the sight of her—and then my throat constricts. I stand abruptly, shaking.

My mother.

She's exactly the same as I remember—long, dark hair. Large, blue eyes. Berry pink lips. Thinner than before, and perhaps a bit older, too, but still beautiful.

Her eyes—I expected empty, vacant eyes. But they brighten when she sees me, when she takes me in, and they trail down my body once.

A boy. I was just a boy when she came here. And now?

Her cerulean irises flick back up to mine, tears welling as she smiles.

"Ash," she whispers, holding a hand out. "You're so big," she adds, her voice catching.

Her voice—the same, low, soothing voice I remember as a kid.

My mother was my best friend. My fortress against my father. My safeguard. She tried to get away a couple of times, but he always managed to drag her—*us*—back. He knew how to play her, how to perfect his words just so. And then she got pregnant, and my father...

My father lost it.

I know now that it was not his child, and to this day, I

still don't know whose baby it was. As a teenager, I understood enough of the situation, and for a long time, I was angry at her. For having an affair, for getting pregnant, and then for not being strong enough to endure the hormonal shifts after the miscarriage. My father was keen to fuel my anger. The brainwashing, the gaslighting, turning me against her... it wasn't until recently that I realized how wrong he was.

How wrong I was...

How naive...

I close my eyes, thinking of Samson briefly. Of his mental health struggles, of how he overcame them. I think of Micah and how he wasn't so lucky...

I open my eyes and walk to my mother. Without a word, she pulls me into a tight hug, and we both collapse into a fit of sobs. I clutch the material of her hospital shirt —fisting it tightly as my chest cleaves open.

There is so much she doesn't know—so much she wasn't there for.

My cowardice did this—my fear of seeing her changed. A fear that was unfounded, obviously. My mother kept herself sane here, kept her spirit alive somehow. For *five* years.

When we pull apart and wipe our faces, she smiles and touches my face.

Love. There is only love in her eyes.

"I'm sorry it took me so long," I mutter, blinking a few times and sniffing. "I wanted to come earlier, but—"

"Sweetie," she says, her voice soothing and calm. "You don't need to explain yourself." She pulls me into another hug, and I smile against her, against the smell of lilacs and lavender—a smell I'd forgotten until this very moment.

I can't remember the last time I felt this...happy.

Somehow, seeing her has given me a taste of reassurance—like everything will somehow be okay.

It will all be okay. If she could endure five years in isolation, away from me? I can do anything.

"I'm sure you have so much to tell me," she says, her voice upbeat.

How does she do it? Is she putting on a brave face? I can't even fathom the strength it must take if so. And then I think, of course she's putting on a brave face.

And the thought is so admirable, so...potent with love... I hug her again.

This time, I don't let go for a very, very long time.

❧ 17 ❧

BRIAR

I spend all week tirelessly introducing myself to the other students at Ravenwood. Samson comes with me, and together we attempt to appeal to the masses. The first day, I buy a bunch of cookies and hand them out. People are reluctant, of course, but soon, I get a small smile from a few people. The next day, I joke with a group of seniors about our pre-calculus teacher, and I swear I see a flicker of surprise on their faces. As we walk away, Samson squeezes my hand.

"Look at you," he muses, smiling. "A true Queen, through and through."

The third day—Wednesday—I notice several people placing their votes in the ballot box. Swallowing, I decide to make flyers after school. Ledger—who is a very talented artist, it turns out—helps me create a fun campaign slogan. *Give Me The Crown, And Together We'll Rule—Give Me The*

Crown, And I Won't Let Your Down. Vote Briar Monroe and Samson Hall for Homecoming Royalty!

Ledger draws an ornate crown, and then a caricature of Samson and I that has us all howling with laughter.

But it works—because on Thursday, people are stopping to read the flyers I've placed all around the ballot boxes. I even see a few people changing their votes last minute. Only when Scarlett and Jack walk by do I second guess myself. Especially when they don't make eye contact with me.

My mom helps me bake cookies that night, and Hunter helps me decorate them. We have way too much fun, and after my mom goes to bed, he hoists me up onto the kitchen counter, screwing me senselessly—and quietly, so we don't wake our parents.

By Friday, I feel confident as I distribute the cookies with Samson, and together we make alliances with the jocks, the drama kids, the math club... People begin to wave at us, and somehow, even just for the week, the energy is different. I have to hope it's permanent—that the homecoming ceremony is just the start of people opening up to the idea of befriending the Kings.

And when I leave campus on Friday afternoon, my arm looped with Samson's, we both seem to exhale as we walk with the guys to our cars.

"Think it'll work?" he asks me, smirking.

I shrug. "I hope so."

If nothing else, this campaign was a welcome distraction, because I've hardly thought about Cam all week.

❧ 18 ❧

BRIAR

I pull the gown over my head, the white, beaded material clinging to every curve. Looking in the mirror, I swallow the lump in my throat when I remember the last time I got dressed up for something, and how I got to spend time with Scarlett and Jack. Now, it's just me—with no one to help get me ready. Because of that, I've opted for minimal makeup—just filling in my brows, adding a bit of shimmering bronzer, and a nude lipstick. I reach down and step into the silver, strappy sandals, admiring the dress and the beautiful, soft material. It's 1920s inspired, with a V-neck and a slight flare at my knees—but form-fitting everywhere else. The back is loose and hanging, leaving my back bare nearly down to my ass. My hair is simple, mostly because my mom helped me pull it into a braided crown.

"Fit for a queen," she'd said.

She'd been so excited to find out I was vying for

Homecoming Queen—thanks to Andrew telling her, obviously—because that was once her title, too. And since I was never into sports or cheerleading or anything she loved as a teenager, it made her happy to see me follow in her footsteps.

I grab my black clutch and head out of my room, closing my door behind me. I hear people downstairs, and I know the guys are all here to take me to school. In California, homecoming dances were a casual affair compared to prom. But the guys told me this would be akin to a wedding, so to dress accordingly. As I descend the stairs, everyone quiets, and my mom walks up to me, brushing a strand of hair off my face.

"You look beautiful, hon," she says, her voice fraught with emotion.

"Thanks, Mom," I say, giving her a half smile.

When I look over her shoulder, my breathing hitches as my eyes land on Hunter's. He's in a dark green dress shirt and dark grey slacks, with a black leather belt and matching boots. His leather jacket hangs over one of his arms. Ash is next to him, in a black shirt with the sleeves rolled up, and black pants. He's wearing high-top red Converse. My eyes flit to Ledger, who is in a light pink shirt and navy pants. He's also wearing Converse, but his are bright pink. I glance at Samson, and he's wearing a white shirt, black pants and dress shoes, and his tie...

Smiling, I walk up to him and reach out for his tie. It's white with the same beads as my dress.

"How did you know?" I ask, smirking.

He smiles down at me, and my heart nearly skips a beat. "I asked Hunter to do some reconnaissance for me so that we could match."

My throat constricts, but I tamp down the emotions as I turn to face the others.

"You look great, Briar," Hunter says, and then my mom's camera flash goes off.

"Sorry," she mutters, fidgeting with it. "Hunter and Briar—can I get a picture of you two first? Maybe for the mantle?"

Oh, god.

I pull my lips to one side and try not to laugh as Hunter and I stand awkwardly next to each other. His fingers barely brush mine, sending sparks flying up my arm. My nipples harden beneath the thin fabric of my dress, and I bite my lower lip as Mom takes a few different pictures from different angles. Andrew is already at homecoming, and my mom is heading over later, if she feels better—her words, not mine.

"Thank you," she says, giving us both a knowing smile. "You make a beautiful couple."

My breathing stills, and before she can say more, Ledger interrupts us.

"Okay, the bus is here. We should go."

I smile at him gratefully, and Ash walks me out the front door, his hand on my lower back. "You look positively edible tonight, Briar," he purrs, a hand moving down my exposed back.

The feel of his warm, calloused fingertips on my sensitive skin sends shivers down my limbs, and I crane my neck to look up at him. "Thank you, Ash."

We climb into the party bus, and I have to laugh when I see a disco ball and flashing lights inside. As I find a seat, Hunter approaches with two champagne glasses and hands me one, and we click glasses before taking a large sip of the bubbly, sweet liquid. The other guys take seats in the back.

The bus begins to move, and loud pop music sounds in the speakers. "Who booked this thing anyways?" I snort. "And how did you manage champagne?"

He grins and takes another sip of champagne. "We paid the driver a lot of money not to ask about the champagne bottles we provided."

Ah. That explains it.

I shrug. "I've never been to a dance before. We had them in California, but they never interested me."

"So there was no losing your virginity at prom?" he murmurs, a feline smile on his beautiful lips.

I shake my head. "No, more like joints and blankets and bonfires on the beach."

He laughs. "That sounds fun, too."

"I can't imagine anyone from Ravenwood actually enjoying the public school system," I retort. Hunter's face falls slightly, and I remember something Jack told me on my first day. "Your dad almost sent you to one, didn't he?"

He's quiet for a second, and then he looks out the window. "Last year, after Micah... After he died, my father started to get very sensitive about my reputation. For a good reason. I certainly pushed his buttons more than I should've. And one day, after he found out about me skipping class, he threatened to kick me out and send me to Jefferson High. Anyways, we've since worked through it. I can't wait to graduate, to get the fuck out of this town and see what the world has to offer."

"And write the next Great American Novel," I joke, brushing my shoulder against his.

He smiles, and I swear I see the faintest hint of a blush

on his cheeks. "Perhaps."

As the bus pulls into the Ravenwood parking lot, my pulse speeds up. Climbing out, I let Samson take my arm as we walk through the gate toward the gymnasium.

"You ready?" he asks, giving me a feline smile.

I shrug and shake my head. "No. You?"

He sighs. "Same."

The cluster of people hanging out near the entrance parts down the middle as we walk up, and most of them stop talking as we walk into the gym. A few of them wave at Samson and me.

That must be a good sign.

I tighten my grip on my clutch, and my anxiety causes my nerves to fly every which way.

I spot Scarlett and Jack sitting with some juniors I don't know, and when I smile at them, they give me a small, sad smile back before turning around. I ignore the ache in my chest. I wish I could talk to them—I wish they understood.

The five of us claim a table up front, and Samson and I sit down as we look around. Hunter, Ash, and Ledger all murmur something about getting drinks and food, and Samson takes my hand and kisses it once—gently.

"Relax," he purrs. "It's a dance, and everyone is here to watch their Queen."

I roll my eyes. "A title I have not earned yet," I remind him, and we both laugh.

"Perhaps. But they'd be stupid not to see you for what you are." Looking around, he pulls a flask out from his coat pocket. "Want some liquid courage?"

I grin. "You read my mind."

When the guys return, we pour vodka into the punch,

and it's not a terrible way to spend the night. After a few minutes, I feel much lighter and happier, and the impending crowning ceremony feels a lot more doable now. The guys even manage to get me onto the dance floor, and to my delight, a few students laugh at us as we flail about. Laugh—not scowl. Like maybe they don't completely hate us after all. Just as a new song starts, Darian—the guy who befriended me at Ash's party a few weeks ago—taps the microphone.

"All right, Ravenwood Academy! It's that time of the night where we announce our King and Queen." I look up at him, holding my breath. Samson takes my hand and squeezes it once.

One chance to blast apart the reputation of the Kings. One chance to show everyone that they're not brutes. The only question is, did my efforts pay off? I don't even care about winning—the crown is futile. But it would be evidence that perhaps the tides are turning.

Darian takes his place at the podium and clears his throat.

"It was really close this year, but I'm happy to announce our newest homecoming King and Queen. Please give it up for Samson Hall and Briar Monroe!"

My stomach bottoms out with relief, and I grin. There's a polite applause, and Samson takes my hand and laces his fingers with mine, squeezing me once. There's some upbeat music playing, and when I look out into the crowd, I notice that no one seems pissed off that we've been crowned. A few people clap again as we walk up, and I give them appreciative smiles.

Darian gives both of us a quick hug, and then he places two plastic crowns on our heads as we face the crowd. I feel Samson pull a sash over my head, and several people take pictures with their phones. I swallow the nerves threating to come up as bile, and my hands shake as I wave to the general student body. The shock of winning prohibits me from truly celebrating, but holy crap, we did it!

"We did it, little lamb," Samson whispers into my ear. It must look very intimate because a few people whoop.

It's hard to see with the lights shining down on us, and I hold a hand over my eyes as I smile. I look for Scarlett and Jack, but I don't see them. Maybe they'll realize that we're not so awful now—maybe they'll see that enough people voted for us, and perhaps the reputations the Kings have is old news. I continue looking for them. *We did it. Samson and I—we did it! My hard work paid off, and perhaps now we can begin dismantling the hierarchy at Ravenwood Academy.*

My eyes flit to someone leaning against the back wall, and—

No.

My blood freezes in my veins, and I suddenly can't breathe. I let out a faint gasp, reaching for Samson and squeezing his hand.

Cam.

Squinting, I watch as Cam smiles at me—dressed in a suit so that he fits in—and then he turns around and goes through one of the doors in the gym.

"Briar," Samson says, his voice concerned. "What's wrong?" The class president is talking into the microphone, and then he holds it out to me. I don't have a chance to tell Samson as I wrap my clammy hands around the black metal.

"Thank you so much, everyone," I say, clearing my throat. *He ruined this—I had so much to say to everyone, and he ruined it.* "I hope you all have a wonderful night."

There are a few snickers as I pass the mic to Samson, and he watches me with concern. I widen my eyes and gesture for him to hurry.

"Thanks, everyone!" A large group of girls in back screams, fanning themselves as they clap excitedly.

Okay, well that's new.

As the class president escorts us off the stage, I grab ahold of Samson's arm and squeeze. When we're out of earshot, he turns to me.

"What's wrong?"

My voice is shaking as I tell him. "Cam is here. He went through the back door. But he's h-here, Samson," I stammer.

How did he get through security? How did no one recognize him?

Before I can say more, he takes my hand and stalks to our table. The other guys must know something is amiss because they all jump up.

"Cam's here," Samson growls.

"He went through the back door," I explain, pointing toward the back. "Like thirty seconds ago."

Ash is the first one to bolt, and Hunter and Ledger follow. The three of them jog to the door, and Samson turns back to me, squeezing my hand.

"You should stay—"

"Absolutely fucking not," I cry, letting go of his hand and dropping my arms to my side.

I see the resignation on his face as he nods—the surrender. "All right. Let's go get him."

❦ 19 ❦

SAMSON

Our feet slap against the linoleum of the hallway, the darkness overwhelming as we slow our pace, quieting. The only thing I hear now is our ragged breathing. Ledger and Ash check each classroom, throwing the doors open, one after the other, until we get to the end of the hallway. Hunter is hiding Briar behind him, and I almost laugh at the ridiculousness. He's gone. Why would he stick around? If someone saw him, if someone recognized him...

He'd gone back to wherever he came from—whatever shithole lair he'd been living in.

I curl my fists so hard that my nails dig into my palms.

"Let's check the parking lot," Briar says, pointing to the quad—and the parking lot beyond it.

I nod. "Yeah. Good idea."

We open the door and wander into the quad. Out of the corner of my eye, I see Hunter throw his leather jacket over Briar. An arm around her shoulder, he holds her close to him as we quickly walk to the parking lot. There are a few cars here, and some of the party buses and limos are waiting around, clustered together as if in commiseration. But I don't see anything that would indicate Cam or the car he used to get here.

I sigh and run a hand through my hair. Why did I run? I should've followed him that day in the store. If I had, we wouldn't be here now. Instead of enjoying homecoming, we're worried, on edge...and scared.

Ash sighs and sits on the curb, and Ledger and I sit on either side of him. Briar and Hunter sit on the asphalt—Briar in Hunter's lap—as we all stare out into the dark night, quiet.

Briar speaks first. "I'm not crazy. I saw him—"

"I know," I growl. "Now I don't feel so crazy. I've been going over that day in my head, and I've been questioning myself for weeks now—trying to figure out if I actually saw him, or if it was all in my head."

Her throat bobs as she nods. "You're not crazy."

"I still think we should notify the police." Hunter rubs his jaw. "Let them continue the search."

Briar shakes her head. "They'll wonder why it took us so long to say something."

"But we could say we saw him tonight—"

"Hunter." Briar's voice is sharp. "What are they going to do? They're already tracking his credit cards, his car, bank accounts, everything. He's an escaped inmate. The whole country is on alert. He's eluding the FBI, for fuck's sake—and the guy your dad hired to find him. The only thing it's going to do is make my mom more nervous. She'll never let me leave the house."

·He grimaces. "I understand your reasoning, but I think it'll be a huge help to know he's been spotted here—in Greythorn. We need help now, Briar. Before, it was a shot in the dark, but now? He's hunting you. And we need as many people on our side as possible."

"I'm going to find him," Ash muses, lethal darkness passing over his face. "Even if I have to knock on every door in Greythorn."

"We'll find him." Ledger rests his chin on his hand as he blows out an exasperated breath.

Briar yelps. "Hunter...what if it *was* him following us last weekend?"

Hunter swallows, taking in her words. "Yeah...it's definitely a possibility."

We're quiet for a few minutes, the defeat permeating the air. For a second, I thought maybe we'd at least get a glimpse of his car, or some sort of clue—maybe even confront him, which might've been stupid. But it would've been something. It would've felt productive—would've been a step forward.

"Also, the suit," Briar murmurs. "He was wearing a suit." Her eyes snap to mine. "Maybe we could talk to the suit rental shop in town?"

I nod. "Yeah. We'll start there tomorrow."

Briar sighs. "You're right, though. I think we need to tell the authorities."

"Soon," Ledger insists. "He could be planning on attacking tonight."

"Yeah," Ash chimes in. "Tonight. Before the party. We go to the police station with what we know."

"And after," Ledger adds, standing and helping Ash and me up. "We can go get fucked up at my party."

I'd nearly forgotten about the party at Ledger's house.

We head back inside the gymnasium to grab Briar's purse, and then we walk out—Hunter on Briar's right side, and me on her left. I see Scarlett and Jack staring at us, and I give them both a small, reassuring smile.

20

Briar

It all feels too familiar—the bright lights, the cops, the interrogation room. The guys don't really have any additional information since I'm the only one who saw him. For now, we leave out that we knew he was here. I don't want to incriminate Samson or get him in trouble for not saying something earlier. But the sheriff—an older man with dark hair—looks resigned and tired by the time I'm done recounting tonight. I'm sure having one of America's most wanted in his normally safe, sleepy town is not what he signed up for.

"Thank you for telling us," he says as he walks me out of the station. The guys are waiting for me outside—the party bus still idling. "We'll find him, Ms. Monroe."

I fucking hope so.

By the time we take the party bus to Ledger's house, we've decompressed a bit, shaking the events of the night off. The two glasses of champagne the guys handed me didn't hurt. A few people are already parked outside his gate, vaping and laughing while leaning against their cars. Ledger hops out and unlocks his front door, a wicked grin on his face as he greets the early partygoers. We follow closely behind. I try not to smile as a few people smile at him—actually *smile*.

None of them make direct eye contact, but it's a start.

I walk up to the Huxley house with Samson. I get inside the ornate mansion, and I don't expect what I see.

"This is... Wow."

It's dark and moody, and the foyer is covered in crosses of all sizes. The walls are a dark grey, and as I continue farther past the entrance, my eyes take in the gothic furniture, dark walls, and religious undertones through the house. The couch is white and pristine—the desk in the office is made of clear lucite. It's strange—instead of stylish, it's...eerie. I look up and behold iron chandeliers hanging from the ceilings. It almost feels like a medieval dungeon.

"It's a lot," Samson muses. "Like we told you, his parents are freaks. Religious nuts that are so far gone down the rabbit hole, you truly wonder how they're still functioning."

I swallow, and more people file in. "So he normally hosts parties here?"

Samson nods, walking me into the kitchen. Ledger is busting out the alcohol, laying everything out on the large island. There is beer, wine, cocktails, canned drinks, you name it...

"Yeah. His parents are gone most weekends at public

speaking events—mostly at religious schools—preaching about premarital sex and sin," he adds, laughing.

Hunter and Ash begin pushing all the furniture to the side, leaving large spaces in the center of each room.

"So if I remember correctly, Ledger's brother is older, twenty-four? And he's a tattoo artist in Boston?"

Samson places an arm around my shoulder, murmuring into my ear. "Yep. Both Ledger and Silas rejected this life from very early on," Samson muses, his lips brushing against my ear.

Right. I remember now. "And that's how Ledger got his ink?"

Samson nods. "His parents aren't home that often, but when they are, they don't really acknowledge Ledger, or his tattoos. They allow him to live here and pay rent, which is fucked up, but they gave up on their kids a long time ago. Silas and Ledger are close, though. So at least they have each other."

I shake my head, imagining how awkward it must be to cohabitate with people who are so unlike you—people who are supposed to be your greatest role models.

Ledger appears, handing me a water. "Thanks," I murmur, taking a sip. "Your house is a vibe," I joke, and he smiles. Samson excuses himself to help Hunter and Ash get the house ready for a rager.

"You think *this* is a vibe? I should show you the chapel."

"Chapel?" I'd completely forgotten about that.

He pins me against the kitchen island and places his hands on either side of me, gripping the counter.

"Chapel," he confirms, his eyes narrowing, focusing on my lips before flitting up to my eyes. "Come on. Let's go."

Before I can respond, he reaches for my hand and drags me to a doorway, opening it and pulling us down the dark, narrow stairway. What kind of person would put a chapel in a basement? Chills work their way down my spine the farther we descend, and then my feet hit stone, and Ledger hits a switch.

The room—the chapel—before us is plain with wood-paneled walls, a couple rows of wooden pews, an ornate runner that leads to the wooden altar. Behind the altar looms a giant cross, overshadowing the entire room. On either side of the cross, black wings carved of dark wood flare out on either side. And the lighting comes from two iron sconces on the wall, giving our shadows a moody, haunted feel.

He dims the light and walks up to the altar. There's a small podium there with a Bible, and two ornate candelabras extend on either side.

They look like devil's horns.

"We spent many days in here, punished by our parents for something any normal child would do, like fighting with my brother or taking the Lord's name in vain," Ledger starts, looking up at the cross. In his collared shirt and dress pants, he looks so...distinguished. His eyes look at me over his shoulder. "I once spent three hours down here because I didn't say 'yes, sir,' to my father. By the time I was eight, I knew I never wanted to be anything like them."

I move toward him, my heels sinking into the plush, Persian carpet leading to the altar.

"I don't blame you," I say, taking Hunter's jacket off. I cross my arms, trying not to smile as he pulls his lower lip between his teeth. "How many girls have you brought down here?" I joke, cocking my head. I run a finger along the wood of the pew.

He smirks. "You're the first," he murmurs, stepping down from the altar.

I suck in a breath as he walks over and moves his large hands to my shoulders, slipping his fingers underneath the fabric of my dress. Slowly—so, so slowly—he slips the dress down my shoulders, causing it to slip off entirely. The heavy beading falls and gathers at my feet. I step out of my dress and shoes and place my palms on his chest in nothing but a black lace bustier and a matching thong.

He growls, studying me, then grabs my waist and pulls me into him, tipping my chin up as he places a kiss on my mouth. I melt—my body relaxing against the warmth of his body.

"Lie down," he commands, and when I look up at him, his tongue ring slips between his teeth briefly as he toys with it.

"Where?"

He nudges his jaw toward the altar, and I lie down facing the cross. This feels....*so* sacrilegious. Blasphemous. But in a way...so right. Ledger runs a hand through his blonde hair as he slowly unbuttons his shirt, one button at a time, his eyes on me.

"Last weekend was fun," he remarks, tilting his head as he studies me. "But I've been waiting to fuck you alone— all by myself—for weeks now, so I apologize in advance if you're sore tomorrow." I open my mouth to respond, but he interrupts me. "I want you to think of me—and only me—when one of the other guys fucks you tomorrow. That I got here first. Just tomorrow. And then I can be a good boy and go back to sharing."

My breathing turns heavy, my chest rising and falling rapidly. Without taking his pants off, he walks onto the altar and leans over me—his shirt unbuttoned, his hair falling in front of his face. The cross behind him makes it look as though the horizontal beam is attached to his shoulders, holding him up, the painting giving him the illusion of wings. I swallow as he removes his belt, tugging it out of his pant loops and wrapping it around the base of the podium behind me.

"Arms up, Briar," Hunter growls, and I move my arms above my head so that my fingers graze the wood of the podium. I gasp as he loops the belt around each wrist, securing my hands together above my head.

"Ledger—"

"Let me admire you," he mumbles, sitting back and drinking me in with his eyes. A sound so low I don't hear it —instead, I *feel* it—reverberates through me as his thumb moves to the band of my thong. "These," he grumbles, looking down at me. "I love these." He slips a finger inside, the heat of his skin cool against my burning flesh. He removes my thong, and I help him by shimmying my hips. His hands move up then, unclasping my bustier at the front so that my breasts spring out. "Fuck," he rasps.

He lowers his head, and I squeeze my eyes shut and arch my back as his tongue flicks against my taut, sensitive nipples. I let out a moan, thrashing against the belt as the metal stud of his tongue ring knocks against my skin. When I open my eyes, he's sitting back again. This time, he unzips his pants, reaching out and freeing his giant, thick cock. I begin to tremble with anticipation as I watch him stroke it.

He knocks my legs apart with his knee, causing me to

gasp as he lowers himself on top of me, the heavy weight of his body against my chest. I feel the tip of his shaft against my opening—feel the warmth there. My eyes meet his, and I take in his tanned skin, his clear, blue eyes that look indigo in the dark chapel. He swallows, and his throat bobs—the only sign of nervousness he shows before thrusting into me.

Something splinters apart as he drives into me, and I scream, both in pain and pleasure. We've had sex before, but I was much more warmed up last time—had four guys fawning over me. This feels...different. Softer, somehow. *Reverent.* My eyes don't leave Ledger's as he drives into me again, and this time, I hiss.

"Am I hurting you?" he asks, his gaze fierce.

I shake my head, and the belt buckle clicks against the wooden floor of the altar. Ledger whispers something, but it's unintelligible. It sounds like some sort of prayer, and the thought spurs me on. I throw my head back, close my eyes, and arch my back as he drives into me—the pain surrendering to pleasure that seeps into every pore, every crevice deep inside of me.

When I snap my eyes open, his face is flushed, his mouth pulled tight. Reaching up to one of my breasts, he twists my nipple—roughly—driving into me with such force that I gasp.

"Is that too much?" he whispers, his voice frenetic. He's completely overtaken with something primal—his pupils are dilated all the way, and he's panting.

"No," I breath, swallowing. "I like it."

He gives me a lecherous smile then, and clamps his fingers on both nipples, twisting viciously. He's thrusting into me with such force now that I can feel my body squeeze him, tightening with every movement.

I scream—and then I unexpectantly come apart.

Gasping for air, my orgasm rips through me—every taut muscle releasing in wave after wave of pleasure so potent and strong that I buck against the belt. The clanking permeates the silence of the chapel, and I feel my body completely succumb to his as he roars, his climax sliding through him just as quickly as mine did.

"Holy fuck," he pants, pulsing inside of me.

Our breathing slows as we both still, and he drops his head to mine, kissing me softly—first on my lips, and then on each cheek, and then my eyelids. It feels intimate, and I swallow as he looks down at me.

"Wow," I whisper, and he unbuckles my wrists. They spring free, and I shake them out. I see red marks on them, and I try to hide my smile.

He said I would be sore tomorrow, and I have to wonder if he was rough on purpose.

Neither of us says anything for several minutes as he collapses beside me on the altar. I assume there are more partygoers upstairs, considering the music and voices have gotten progressively louder over the last minute or two. Ledger faces me, smiling, then gestures the sign of the cross.

I swat his arm playfully, and we both laugh for what feels like hours. Finally, he helps clean me up, holding me as I slip back into my dress and shoes, and we head upstairs to the party.

21

BRIAR

I spend the next morning recounting my night with my mom and Andrew. My mom is totally freaked out about Cam, but Andrew reassures her that he'll help bolster police activity in the area to keep an eye out. After a late breakfast, I tell them I'm headed to Jack's house.

A few minutes later, I pull behind Jack's BMW i3. I look down at the directions on my phone, squinting against the bright autumn sun as I compare the address on the school roster with the address on my phone. Is it a requirement that every person in Greythorn have luxury cars and pretentious houses? I lock the Subaru, walking up to the ornate front door and knocking. A couple minutes and two knocks later, I'm just about to turn around when a woman opens the door, and I know instantly that she's Jack's mother.

"Hi," I say, my voice uncertain. "I'm Briar. I'm here to

see Jack?"

She gives me a warm smile. Beautiful—younger than I imagined, with porcelain skin and bright red hair, the exact shade of Jack's.

"He's actually with Scarlett," she says, her voice throaty and low. "He should be home soon if you want to come inside." Studying me, she tilts her head to the side. "You're Andrew's stepdaughter, right? I think he mentioned your name to me." She must see my look of confusion because she continues. "I work as an attorney, and we recently updated some documents for the Academy," she explains. "How are you finding Greythorn? I hope it's not too soul-sucking," she jokes.

I huff a laugh. "It's fine."

She seems nice, and I feel at ease. And it seems that she has Jack's sense of humor.

"We must have you all over for dinner sometime—"

"Briar?"

I twist around, and Jack is standing there with Scarlett. They're watching me with careful concern—they don't know why I'm here.

"You're welcome to come in with Jack if you want. I think I hear my phone ringing. So wonderful to meet you, Briar," Jack's mom says politely before turning and walking away.

I'm left with the two of them, and neither of them move.

"I was hoping we could talk," I say quietly.

"Briar—"

"No," I interrupt Scarlett, holding a hand out. "I really need to talk to you. There are things you don't know about me, and—"

Jack pulls Scarlett past me. By the time I turn to face them, Jack has a hand on his front door, ready to slam in my face. "You made your choice, Briar. We get it. But it's not like we can change your mind."

He moves to shut the door, but just before it clicks shut, I call out— "I was raped!"

The door pauses.

"In California. He was my mom's boyfriend at the time, and he... he raped me. There was a trial, and he was sentenced to thirteen years."

The door slowly opens again, and they both watch me with crossed arms.

"None of them are like their reputations. They're caring, compassionate, kind. That day in a quad? I said something about men raping women, remember? And they stopped. They *stopped*. None of them ever tried anything shady, despite being jerks the first few days. And they... they look out for me. Because Cam—the man who raped me—escaped prison three and a half weeks ago."

I leave out the part about Cam being in Greythorn. The authorities know, my mom and Andrew know, and there's no reason to worry anyone else.

Scarlett's throat bobs. "I'm sorry about what happened to you. I didn't realize..." She trails off. "And you're... sleeping with all of them?"

I nod. "It just sort of happened."

Jack looks at me, standing up straighter. "How does that work, exactly?" His voice is still a bit skeptical, but there's also a hint of curiosity.

I shrug. "I don't know. They all offer something different. And they aren't planning on making me choose one of them to be exclusive with. We're just kind of having fun," I explain. "It feels normal. Natural. Like this was always meant to happen."

"They never really publicly dated anyone," Scarlett adds, dropping her hands to her side. "I mean, I'm sure they messed around. Girls threw themselves at the Kings every single day. And of course Samson dated Micah, and Ash fooled around with Jack—"

"Hey," Jack whines.

"Sorry, Ash *dated* Jack," she clarifies.

"It was three months," he says defensively.

"My point is," I start, trying not to smile as they both lower their arms. "They've been wonderful. I'm not saying you have to forgive them, Samson especially. But he loved Micah—he told me they were in love, and that everything was a misunderstanding."

They look at each other before looking at me. "And Medford?" Scarlett asks.

I tilt my head. "It was Ash's idea, because his father abuses him. He wanted to send a message."

"I knew it," Jack hisses, his voice cruel. "He used to have bruises on his ribs. "But every time I asked, he'd change the subject."

"Is that why Christopher is in prison?" Scarlett asks.

I nod. "Ash recorded the last time it happened and sent it to the police."

They look between themselves, and then at the ground. Scarlett looks up at me through her lashes.

"Are you happy?" she asks.

I swallow. "Happier than I've ever been."

"I still don't trust them," she murmurs. "But I trust you." And then she hugs me, and I sag with relief.

I've missed them—and even though the Kings are fine friends, sometimes I just need a break from the angst.

I put my arms around them as we head inside, and Jack's mom makes us a delicious meal. I learn that both his parents are attorneys, and, like most of the kids here, Jack and his family come from old money. When we finish eating, we head up to Jack's room, which is filled with paperbacks of his favorite books—mostly paranormal romance. As we catch up on life, I tell them a bit about the guys. When I finish giving them a very brief overview of our camping trip, Scarlett gasps.

"I'm, like, jealous in a weird way?"

I snort. "I thought you didn't like men."

She shrugs. "I don't—but who wouldn't love being worshipped like that?" she squeals.

"Scarlett is right," Jack muses, his handsome face stoic and serious. "I am definitely jealous."

"And Ash?" I ask, my real question unspoken.

He gives me a small smile. "Ash is...*was*...the love of my life. But it was always unrequited."

I swallow.

Ash—the brooding bad boy with skeletons in his closet and a heart of gold.

Every time I think about which one I would choose if I had to, it's impossible.

"Real question though..." Scarlett says, her voice soft. "How does this end?"

I look at them, crossing my arms. "I have no idea."

We're quiet for several seconds until my phone beeps, and when I look down, my pulse quickens.

"Oh, my god," I whisper, a smile playing at my lips. "They released Hannah Greythorn."

🎕 22 🎕

BRIAR

I'm restless as I pace our large living room, waiting for Hunter to get home. He'd gone with Ash to pick Hannah up, and I swallow when I think about what Ash must be going through right now—to be reunited with his mother, to see her outside the sterile walls of the psychiatric hospi-tal. The complicated, *loving* relationship they had—regard-less of Hannah's affair, the pregnancy, and ultimately having to choose his father over his mother. He was a kid —a *child*. How was he supposed to choose? Especially with Christopher Greythorn whispering horrible things in his ear.

It was no wonder Ash turned out the way he did— sometimes crass and insecure, but loyal as all get out. He'd had his mother ripped from him, had his family torn apart. He lashed out—made a show of being strong, unbreakable.

But maybe he was the one who needed the most care.

Hunter pulls into the driveway, and I throw the door open. I'll never get over his refined, effortless style and moody disposition. He might as well have been straight out of my fantasies—dark, brooding, dangerous.

"Is Ash okay?" I get out, crossing my arms as he walks into the study.

Hunter nods, leaning against the desk. "Yeah, he seemed okay. Hannah looks exactly the same, too—so whatever she had to endure in that place didn't break her spirit."

"That's good, right?"

He shrugs. "I think only time will tell. But they both seemed happy. Christopher had fortunately kept her things —so she doesn't really have to settle in all that much. And her friends are bringing them dinner for the next week or so. They're going to need to learn how to live with each other again. So much has changed..."

I look down for a few seconds before I respond. "What will happen to Christopher?"

Hunter's dark eyes find mine. There's a hint of sadness in them. The media speculates he'll remain in jail, bit I want to hear it from Hunter. "Christopher will be in jail for a long time." Something about the way he says it—full of conviction—sends chills down my body. He continues. "Ash caught him on camera. Even though Ash is eighteen, it ruined his career. There were...other things...Ash may have secured him a spot at MCI-Norfolk for many years to come."

I'm quiet as I look out the window, taking in his words. How strange must it be to walk back into your house after five years... I'm about to reach for him when he tugs me into his hard body.

"Where are you going in that tight, little outfit?" he growls, trailing a finger down my chest, down the Lycra fabric of my sports bra. His fingers slip into the waistband of my leggings, and he lets out a low snarl.

I twist my lips to the side, pushing him away playfully. "I was going to go on a jog."

He smiles down at me. "Briar Monroe jogs?"

I laugh. "I don't know. I was so on edge last weekend after that car followed us... I thought maybe it would be a good way to dispel some of the tension—the nervous energy."

"There are other ways to dispel nervous energy," he states, his voice gravelly.

"Oh really?" I tease, blinking a couple times as his fingers move against my clit. My breath catches when he moves my underwear to the side, thrumming my nub with two fingers. I throw my head back, and his teeth find my neck, biting gently.

"It's going to be a problem if I keep having to refer to you as my sister," he growls, his hot breath against my skin.

I open my eyes and look up at him. Something soft— something profound—passes across his face. He places a gentle kiss on my lips, and at the same time, he thrusts two fingers deep inside of me.

I gasp. "Fuck," I breathe, feathering my tongue along his. I don't even know if we're home alone. What would happen if someone were home? If my mom or Andrew heard us...saw us?

"I'm sick of pretending you don't mean anything to me." He pulls my hips into his. I groan into his mouth as his erection presses against me. "Fuck, Briar," he whispers, his voice shaky. "You drive me fucking wild."

I remove his hand and pivot, hopping onto his large desk. "Show me."

His lips are wet and red from kissing me. His brows furrow slightly as he takes me in. Without breaking eye contact, he unbuttons his jeans, stepping out of them completely as he pulls his Henley over his head.

"What if your—"

"I don't give a shit anymore," he growls, stroking his mammoth cock. "I'm going to go crazy if I don't fuck you right now."

His words send a bolt of electricity through me. The need is evident on his face, the animalistic urge to take me in a place that either of our parents could walk into...

I swallow as I pull my bra off and then my leggings.

There's no foreplay, nothing to indicate he's about to drive into me, until he places one hand on my throat and grabs my hips with the other, moving me onto his cock in one swift motion. I cry out.

"Fuck," he shatters, his mouth open in an 'O'. Plunging into me, he takes me differently today—needy, hungry, greedy. I ignore the heavy ache in my chest as his eyes bore into mine—as his warm hands grip me, as I squeeze my eyes shut.

I'm falling for my stepbrother.

I'm not sure I'm ready for what that means.

Holding me by my neck, he groans with every push into me, the crescendo of our voices getting louder. I open my eyes, and a piece of hair has fallen in front of his face, his eyes narrowed, studying me.

I'm sick of pretending you don't mean anything to me.

I clench around him, my muscles taut and ready to spring free. Hunter circles his hips as he quickens his tempo, his nostrils flaring as he breathes heavily. I meet every thrust, moving my hips with his so that he fills me to the hilt over and over. I expect the motion to start my climax, but it's not his cock inside of me—it's the way his eyes find mine, the way they're completely open, the way he almost looks as emotional as I am... A half-sob, half-moan escapes my lips as I study Hunter—who's eyes are on my face, so fervently tender.

"Look at me. You are mine," he hisses, and then he lets out a roar so loud, it shakes the desk.

Shakes me to the core, like an earthquake.

Something molten breaks free from inside of me.

I'm speechless as the lightest, sweetest climax rips through me unexpectedly, caressing every pore, every molecule. I feel myself soak him, feel it hit the desk, feel him pulse and empty inside of me.

After a few ragged breathes, he helps clean me up. I reach for my clothes, but he grabs my arm and pulls me into him—our naked bodies pressed against each other. His heart is thundering—I can feel it. Our breathing is still irregular, and his fingers contract around my flesh, squeezing me tight, pulling me impossibly close. He kisses the top of my forehead.

"Do you think it was fate? Your mom, my dad..." He runs a hand through his wavy hair.

I pull back and smile up at him. "Maybe. Or maybe it was random, and it could've been any guy with a hot son," I joke, sticking my tongue out.

He laughs, nipping my lower lip with his teeth. Pulling away, he helps me into my clothes, and we walk into the kitchen, grabbing some food and sitting at the breakfast nook together. It's nice—and it feels like...*home.* I wonder how the future will unfold with him, because I sure as hell don't want to let whatever we have go. I never want to stop. The problem is, I can't give up his friends, either. How will this all play out?

I give him a quick goodbye kiss a half an hour later, pulling on my shoes and heading out for a quick jog. As I run down the driveway, the same six words continue running through my mind.

It could always be like this.

It could always be like this.

❧ 23 ❧

LEDGER

I drive left onto the main road, and when I stop at the intersection, I think I'm hallucinating when I see a figure run into the park—a figure that looks a hell of a lot like Briar. But I know her, and I know she'd never be running —for fun, at least. I circle the park, and when I get to the other side, I grin when I see her jogging home, red-faced and looking hot as fuck in her running outfit. I pull next to her, and when she sees me, she rolls her eyes, turning in the other direction to avoid me.

I honk, and she flips me off. I chuckle as I park and get out of the car, jogging up to her.

"Hey," I call out, and she turns to face me.

Wiping her brow, she sighs. "Great. The last person I want to see."

I flick my eyes up and down her body, taking in her

curves, the sweat making her cleavage gleam in the sun, the way her dark, curly tendrils are sticking to her hairline... I want to lick it off.

I want to lick every inch of her.

I have a sudden urge to paint her—something that surprises me—to remember her this way forever.

"Why?" I ask, cocking my head.

"Because. You're just going to make fun of that fact that I'm running wrong or something," She shields her eyes from the sun.

"Why would I do that?" I ask, my voice quieter than I intended. "I'm surprised, but I'd never make fun of you."

She growls and throws her arms to the side. "Because, in P.E. that day, you told me how to run correctly. And you made a couple other smartass comments about how hard I was working."

I feel my lips twitch with a smile, but I keep my composure. "And? Is today easier than that day?"

She shrugs, and I can tell she's thinking my words over. "Yeah."

I walk up to her. "I didn't mean for it to sound like I was making fun of you." I smile as I run a finger down her damp arm. Something jumps inside of me at the contact—the feel of her warm, soft skin. The scent of her sweat hitting my nostrils. "I didn't know you ran recreationally," I say, my voice soft. "I'd love to go with you—"

"No," she insists, shaking her head. "You're, like, really good. And I suck."

I laugh. "Briar—"

She turns and jogs away.

"Hey!" I catch up with her and spin her around.

She pulls away from me, and it's then that I see her bottom lip tremble ever so slightly.

"No!" She glares up at me. "I started running last weekend. I had to—I had to burn off some energy. I wasn't sleeping well. I felt like I was hyper-caffeinated all the fucking time. I was going crazy with all that energy." She looks down sheepishly. "I like it, but I'm nowhere near as good as you."

I try to hide my smile as I pull her into me.

"I'll never make fun of someone trying to better their life," I murmur, kissing the top of her head, and she relaxes against me. "If you want, I can help you. If not, that's fine, too." I release her, and she takes a step back, looking at me skeptically.

"I just feel so good after, you know?"

I grin. "I know."

She laughs and shakes her head, looking away. When her eyes find mine again, she looks...relieved. "Fine. I'll let you help me."

I nod. "Okay. Let's start with three days a week. Ease into it a bit. I'll stop by tomorrow morning."

She winces. "What time?"

I walk backwards to my car. "Six."

Sighing, she puts her hands on her hips, and I'm suddenly so acutely aware of how it felt to be inside her Friday night.

"Tomorrow—Monday," I repeat, climbing into my car. "Do you want a ride home?"

She shakes her head. "No. Now I have to get about ten times better before tomorrow, so I should run home."

I laugh. "It doesn't work like that."

She rolls her eyes and turns around. "Goodbye, Ledger," she chirps before jogging off.

I'm still smiling as I drive away, and that's when I realize my mornings are about to get a hell of a lot more interesting.

❧ 24 ❧

BRIAR

My alarm goes off at five forty-five the next morning, and I groan as I snooze for three minutes. By the time I drag my exhausted body out of bed, I'm already regretting this decision. I pull on a pair of jogging pants, a sports bra, a windbreaker, sneakers, and I put my hair into a ponytail. After I brush my teeth, I head downstairs, rubbing my sleepy eyes. Waking this early, for a night owl like me, feels like pure torture. I was smart enough to make some cold brew with milk yesterday, so I pour a cup, leaning against the counter as I drink it down. When my phone dings, alerting me of Ledger at the front door, I grab my keys, a water bottle, and a granola bar.

Opening the door, I can tell he's trying not to laugh when he takes my appearance in. Instead of teasing me, he just smiles.

"Ready?" he asks, and I drink in his running attire. He's

wearing fitted running pants, a sweatshirt, and his hair is pulled back in a headband.

"No," I groan.

"It gets easier, I promise," he says, his voice clear as if he's been awake for hours.

"Oh god, are you a morning person?" I ask as we walk to the sidewalk. I don't see his car, so he must've run here —but he doesn't look out of breath or sweaty at all.

He bends over, stretching his long, muscular limbs. "I love mornings," he replies, grinning.

"Just my luck," I whisper, mimicking his stretching.

"Come on," he says, turning and jogging away.

"Wait, shouldn't we stretch more?"

He laughs, jogging backward. "Can't forget to warm up!" He squints at me with a hint of a smile.

That's exactly what he said to me a couple weeks ago before we messed around in the shower room...

Smartass.

I sigh and jog after him, already regretting every decision that led me here.

❧

An hour later, I'm sprawled on the grass in front of his house, gasping for air.

"It's better if you don't sit or lie down when you're cooling off," he chuckles, pulling me up.

"I...can't...breathe..."

We ran from my house to his—only a little over three miles, but it felt like thirty. I'd never run this far. There were a lot of breaks, and I'm sure I was going at a snail's pace the entire time compared to Ledger. But I did it—and he was very patient with me.

He crosses his arms and looks over at me. He's not even sweating.

Asshole.

"You're testing your endurance," he starts, leaning against the side of his house. "It's just as important as strength training, or sprints. It'll get easier with every run. Maybe you'll be able to run marathons with me by this time next year."

I bark out a laugh. "No way. I could never—"

He places his arms on either side of me, pinning me to the side of the house. Kissing me, he sweeps his tongue into my mouth. I groan, kissing him back, but just as quickly as he'd descended on me, he pulls back, looking at me with hooded, dark eyes.

"Stop being so sure you could never do something, Briar." He nips at my bottom lip with his teeth, pulling on my flesh a bit before letting it go. "Just the fact that you took it upon yourself to *want* to get better means you're one thousand percent stronger than everyone else who just thinks about it. The people who accomplish great things aren't the people who get lucky. They're the people who work their ass off, day in and day out."

I swallow and nod. "Yeah. You're right."

"I know I'm right. Besides, you have the best trainer in the world."

I snort. "And so humble, too."

He laughs. "Come on. We have to hurry or we're going to be late for school."

"Where are you taking me?" I ask, smiling.

"I think we both need to shower off, don't you think?" he asks, winking.

My stomach turns over, and I follow him inside.

Unlike last time, when he took his time screwing me, he collides against my sweaty body, peeling my running clothes off as quickly as possible, his lips on mine as he moves us toward the stairs.

"Where are your parents?" I ask, my voice ragged.

"Fuck if I care," he growls.

"Isn't premarital sex a sin?" I laugh, and he bites my lower lip, spurring me on.

"It is," he muses, grabbing me and throwing me over his shoulder as he scoops our clothes up and glides up the stairs. "Why do you think I like to fuck so much? When something is forbidden, it creates an obsession."

There are no formalities—no explanations—as he turns the shower on in his bathroom. I look around briefly, smiling when I see some darker art and a meticulously organized sink area. He pulls me into the shower. As the steam clings to the clean glass, as he drops to his knees and feasts on me as the water runs down my body.

I should be quiet as he licks and devours me, as his mouth cups me at my apex, sucking. His tongue ring knocks against my clit, and I grip the slippery handle of the shower door, throwing my head back and crying out.

"Ledger," I rasp.

Before I can come, he jumps to his feet and pushes me against the marble wall of the shower. He licks my neck, trails it down my back, and then his tongue flicks between my cheeks. I tense, but he doesn't notice. Not as his hands spread me, as his tongue feasts on the other part of me— the part no one has ever tasted with their mouth. It's odd at first, but so intense that my knees begin to quake. A hand moves between my legs, swirling a finger around my clit, causing me to come so hard that the glass shakes with my cries. Pulse after pulse powers through me, more intense with his mouth on my ass.

And then he claims me—thrusting into my pussy, his chest against my back, driving into me so hard that I leave the floor each time. Grunting, he presses me against the cool marble of the shower, biting my neck at the same time. I realize then that this might be my favorite kind of sex—rough, needy, unkind—in a way that is almost animal-istic. We moan in unison as we climax together. I grip him with each wave, feel him fill me, and then he pulls out, leaving me a trembling mess of nerves.

I'm about to get out of the shower when he grabs my hand, pulling me directly under the stream. He grabs the soap and slowly, ever so slowly, begins to clean me. First my body, then my hair, his large hands making me groan with pleasure as they massage my scalp. He trails kisses along my collarbone, and I have to squeeze my eyes shut as he takes a comb through my hair—it feels *too* intimate, too intense.

My chest aches as he hands me a towel, pulling me into a tight embrace. The towels are even warm from the heated towel rack. I rest my head against his chest.

These boys—these *Kings*—will be my undoing.

25

BRIAR

An hour later, the five of us walk through the gates of Ravenwood Academy together. Unlike before, I feel like I might belong with them—might *actually* be the missing puzzle piece. And the best part is, Scarlett and Jack sheepishly walk over to us, the latter eyeing Ash suspiciously.

"Hey," Ash says, nudging his jaw at Jack.

"Hey, man," Jack answers. "I heard about your mom. I'm glad she's..." he looks down. "You know. I think we're all glad she's out of that place."

Ash swallows and clears his throat. "Thanks."

They begin to walk away, but I lunge forward and grab Scarlett's arm. "You can sit with us."

The silence that follows is uncomfortable for everyone. So many assumptions, so much history, and belief systems that have to be dismantled entirely. But I widen my eyes and look at each of the guys, inferring that this is happening whether they like it or not.

"Um, okay," Scarlett answers, giving Hunter a small smile.

The look he returns is more like a wince, but at least he's trying. I have to give him credit for that.

The seven of us head to the center of the quad, and as Scarlett gives me a silent look of disbelief, the rest of the students at Ravenwood are slightly dumbfounded. Every single person is watching us with bewildered expressions, and I have to bite my tongue to keep from grinning. Even though Samson and I did get crowned homecoming King and Queen, there's still an air of skepticism.

The Kings thought they were getting a Queen, but in actuality, they were getting the woman who would smash their reputations to the ground—the woman who would knock them down from their pedestal, who would humanize them again.

"I think we might be cool again," Samson murmurs into my ear.

I snort. "You guys were always cool. *Too* cool."

When I turn to face him, he's watching me with confusion. "We never thought of ourselves as cool, Briar. We were the outcasts. The people everyone feared, the people no one wanted to associate with." He juts his chin toward Jack and Scarlett, who are seated stiffly next to Ledger. The sight is hilarious. "Why do you think they were so mad at you?"

I shake my head. "Misunderstood, maybe, but everyone came to your parties. You were Homecoming King."

He shakes his head, putting a casual arm over my

shoulder. "There's a difference between popularity and coolness, Briar. Dictators are popular. Lizzo is cool. People want to hang around her. People want to *be* her. People hated us because of who we were." I open my mouth to disagree, but he continues. "I'm not trying to play the victim. But let's say you swim in the ocean with other people, and you start to drown...we weren't the kind of people they would want to save."

I look around, and a few people shake their heads and look away, their gazes harsh and heated. Perhaps I was naïve to think one week would be enough to shatter the rumors. One week—when some of these students have known the Kings since Kindergarten. For some, it's a lifetime of mistrust and skepticism. My work didn't end when I was crowned homecoming Queen. I need to keep going, keep reaching out.

"Because of Micah?" I ask, looking back at Samson.

"Yeah." He sighs, sitting down on a step. I sit next to him, and he leans back on his elbows. "After Micah died, people blamed us. And maybe we were at fault. He was the first outsider we'd let in—the first person besides the four of us, since before I can even remember. One day, they started yelling at us—throwing food at us—and the hatred was evident. They thought we caused him to kill himself, Briar," he says, his voice fraught with emotion. "But we didn't. And that day—people really started to push their boundaries with us. A few people shoved us into lockers. One person spilled acid on Ledger in chemistry—he was fine," he interjects when he sees my horrified expression. "So that night, we decided that instead of fighting against the grain, we might as well embrace it."

"So you played the part," I murmur.

He nods. "We got ahead of the curve. They already hated us, so it didn't matter to us if they hated us even more. Quite frankly, we couldn't care less about what they thought. So, the next morning, Hunter picked on another junior—a guy who kept making snide comments about Micah. He tried to shove Hunter against the lockers, but Hunter was too quick, too smart. To this day, we're still not sure what Hunter said to him, but it was enough for him to back off—for them all to back off. Our rite of passage was complete, and our reputations were solidified. We maintained it over the last year, but until you came along, we just tried to live our lives in peace."

I hug my knees and lean back against the concrete of the center of the quad. "You were just trying to survive," I add. "Playing dead, in a way."

He hums in agreement, and then he's quiet as he looks around. Ash is talking to Scarlett and Jack, and Hunter is deep in conversation with Ledger. His eyes find mine briefly, and he gives me a small smile. "If people stopped hating us, it might not be the worst thing. It's lonely on this throne."

"You're going to have to show them," I retort, smirking. "Show them the side of you that I know."

He makes a face, but then he kisses me quickly—before anyone notices.

The bell rings shortly after that, and as we all walk to our separate buildings, and as Scarlett and Jack flank either side of me, I realize that we may be shaking things up at Ravenwood Academy.

Finally.

✣ 26 ✣

HUNTER

"Ready?" Aubrey asks, zipping her fanny pack as the four of us stand around the front door.

"I'm always ready for Halloween festivities," Briar responds, grinning. "It's my favorite holiday."

I didn't know that.

"Oh, you're going to love how they do it up—it's terrifically spooky," my dad adds, putting an arm around Aubrey.

We lock the door and head to the Subaru, and Briar and I have to actively try not to hold hands as my dad starts the engine.

"Briar used to volunteer at the pumpkin patch back in California," Aubrey muses, chuckling. "She made the cutest witch."

Briar groans. "Mom, please."

Aubrey sends her phone back to me, and when I see the screen, I can't help but grin.

"Is this you?" I ask, laughing.

"Yes," Briar mumbles, her face in her hands.

It's a picture of Briar—at maybe thirteen or fourteen—and she's flashing her braces at the camera, clad in a black robe, a black hat, and black lipstick.

"You do make a cute witch," I add, and she swats my shoulder.

Dad puts on some classic rock, and we're silent as we head up to Salem, Massachusetts for their annual Halloween Fair called Haunted Happenings. My mom used to drag us to it every year, but we haven't been since she died. They have a marketplace where people sell all sorts of creepy things, psychic readings, reenactments of the Salem Witch Trials, yoga at the satanic temple...the list goes on. If Briar loves Halloween, she's going to adore the things we can explore in Salem.

Thirty minutes later, Dad parks in one of the paid lots, and we exit the car. Aubrey and my dad offer to walk around with us, but Briar shoos them away, and we agree to meet in two hours at Settler, one of the nicest restaurants in Salem. Briar and I immediately make out in one of the back allies before she drags me to the gift ship, purchasing half of the store's witch paraphernalia. Afterward, we head down the main road to the courthouse, where an interactive reenactment of one of the trials is taking place—and audience members are being chosen as actors.

I laugh when Briar is instantly found guilty by the actor, and she gives me a droll little smile before playing along, claiming her innocence. The judge—an older man with a beard—declares that she is guilty, and to our surprise, several audience members declare she should be hung, and it's hard not to laugh. When the trial is over, Briar takes a picture with Sheriff Corwin and a couple of the Puritan actors, and we get a picture of the two of us in front of the hanging tree. Laughing, we stumble out and meander through the marketplace.

This—this is *fun.* I can't remember the last time I smiled this much. Maybe never? Not since my mom died. And we certainly haven't been back to Salem since her death. Knowing the last time I was here was with my mom stings a little, but Briar is the antidote to that pain. The feeling of being here is different now, but in a good way. Like we're making new memories. I wouldn't want to be here with anyone else.

We meet up with my dad and Aubrey and then eat our weight in bread and seafood. On the way home, Briar naps against my shoulder, and my dad's eyes find mine in the rearview mirror. I look away; I know what he's thinking.

We're not just stepsiblings.

We're more than that, and it's becoming very evident to those around us.

As we pull into Greythorn, I notice my dad's eyes flicking to the rearview mirror every few seconds—only not at me this time. I look behind us, and there is a black SUV tailgating us. I decide not to wake Briar. She's sound asleep on me, and I don't want to worry her. Dread fills me, because I know who might be following us.

"This person is on my ass," my dad growls. Pulling over, he waits for the car to pass—but it doesn't, instead stopping behind us. "What the hell is their deal?"

I swallow and wipe my sweaty palms on my jeans.

When my eyes find his, I know we're thinking the same thing.

"Just keep driving," Aubrey chimes in. "They're not going to follow us all the way home," she huffs, laughing.

She has no idea.

We pull onto our street. My dad slowly pulls into the driveway, and the black car slows considerably, nearly stopping, before speeding off.

Just like before.

I give my dad a knowing look before waking Briar, gently nudging her as Dad and Aubrey make small talk about grocery shopping for dinner. Once inside, Briar and I head down to the basement, and when we're out of earshot, I turn to her.

"I think Cam was following us again," I say, taking her hand.

"Just now?" She rubs her eyes. "Did he follow us home?"

"Yes." Her face falls, and I can't stand the worry etching onto her face. I'll do *anything* to make it better. "He's not going to touch you here," I growl, hot, angry heat spreading through my limbs. "If he thinks he can touch you here, he will be sorely mistaken."

She nods. "But he knows. He could follow us anywhere now. I didn't even think... We have the same car. The Subaru. He must've seen it, and started following us..."

"Shh," I whisper, kissing her forehead. "It's okay. You're safe. The police know he's here. Our parents know he's here. We're safe, Briar."

"I can't do this anymore," she says, her voice breaking with a sob. "I'm sick of him ruining my happiness. I earned it, Hunter—I fought for that happiness these last nine months. I just want it over with. I want him back in his prison cell, rotting away forever."

"I know. Me too, baby."

Her head snaps up. "What if we lure him out?"

My heart stutters in my chest. "*Lure* him?"

I let her words roll through me, digesting them. "And then what?" I ask, stepping back and crossing my arms. "We let the authorities take over?"

She shrugs. "Yeah. Maybe. I don't know. I'm just tired of always looking over my shoulder, you know?"

"So, what's the plan?"

She looks down, her arms hanging at her sides. "I just want him gone. This was supposed to be the place I started over—the place my mom and I found some semblance of peace. And now he's here, and he's fucking with us...fucking with the people in our life..." She wipes a tear from her cheek. "He's tainting something that should've been my reprieve."

My jaw ticks as we think. "So, we should lure him out of wherever he's hiding, like you said."

She sniffs. "Yeah. But how? I wish we had something like in Salem...some big carnival or something to intrigue him enough to risk being seen. Like homecoming."

I take her hands. "You forget who you're talking to," I drawl, placing a finger under her jaw. "You want a carnival? I'll give you a carnival."

She swallows, but something behind her eyes lights up. "A Halloween carnival. In the main square. No face masks allowed, obviously, because we need to identify him. And we tell the cops about our plan, so they're ready."

I take a step back, grinning. "We're on it, little lamb." Her eyes darken at the nickname. "Consider it done."

27

BRIAR

Scarlett, Jack, and I all spend the next week prepping for the Halloween Carnival—which is taking place on Halloween night, in Greythorn's town square. Halloween is only two weeks away, so we have a lot of work to do before then—things like music, crafts, furniture rentals, permits, sponsors, marketing, costumes... The list goes on. The first thing we decide is what we're going to do—and after the seven of us talk it over, we decide that we'll have a couple of rides, a showing of the *Halloween* movie, food, and trick-or-treating for the kids. We attempt to cover all age ranges, hoping word will spread far and wide. Scarlett and Jack have no idea *why* we're hosting this carnival—they just think we've been planning it all along.

We meet with the officers at Greythorn police station, and the sheriff elects to send twenty officers to the carnival in disguise. Though he isn't totally on board with the idea of *luring* a convicted rapist out of the woods, he agrees it may be our only shot to get to Cam before Cam gets to us.

The food is the easiest to secure for the carnival. Between Scarlett's parents, who own Romancing the Bean, and Samson, who volunteers at his uncle's restaurant, *Enclave*, we have appetizers, dinner, pastries, alcohol, and dessert. The rides are secured by Andrew after one quick phone call to a friend. Ash's mom and my mom volunteer to spread the word by posting advertisements all around the town square, on the campus of Greythorn, and near all the grocery stores. Hunter gives them specific directions— place these posters anywhere that may be visible to anyone and everyone. We all post on social media—Facebook, Instagram, anywhere that we can get the word out.

I also make sure my name and picture are on the poster, and of course the guys want Samson and me to ride the float we arranged—to bolster the Ravenwood Academy spirit, obviously, since we were homecoming King and Queen.

We wanted to lure him in?

Well, we might as well have gone fishing with his favorite bait...

Ledger gets his brother to recommend a band from Boston, and Ash takes care of getting the permits and securing the furniture. Scarlett and Jack begin organizing the decorations, outsourcing to the middle school. We also borrow a lot of things from various haunted houses in the vicinity.

I guess it helps to have connections.

Hunter is in charge of securing sponsors, and with how well his dad is liked, it's not a hard thing to do. We don't necessarily need the money, but a few hundred bucks makes us feel legitimate, and we create a raffle for people to win a weekend away in Salem, all expenses paid.

In a little over a week, we'd taken care of the big things. It's a flurry of school, jogging with Ledger three mornings a week, dinners with my mom, Hunter, and Andrew, a couple of dates with Samson, and random sexual encounters with Ash, usually when he needs to release some steam—like in a broom closet at Ravenwood Academy a few days ago.

I can hardly keep my eyes open when I collapse into bed each night, so when the day before Halloween approaches, I get up early and go for a jog. It's not my morning to jog with Ledger, but I decide to go on my own anyway. I'm up to nearly two miles without wanting to feel like I'm about to die, and I don't want to lose steam.

I jog down the cool, misty street toward the center of town. It's so cold—autumn is in full swing now, and I have to wear a fleece jacket over my running clothes. My nose is numb as I round the corner into the main square, and just as I'm about to stop and stretch, I see Ash sitting on a bench up ahead, facing the park.

When he sees me, he pulls his AirPods out, smiling.

"Briar," he purrs.

"Why are you just sitting on a random bench at seven in the morning?" I ask, looking around. There are quite a few people out—one of the reasons I'm fine jogging in the mornings by myself.

He shrugs as I take a seat next to him. "I couldn't sleep, so I went on a walk, and then I ended up here."

I nod and cross my arms. I don't even realize I'm not out of breath until I feel a trickle of sweat drip down my back. I'm not running marathons yet, but running consistently for a month has really improved my endurance.

"How's it going with your mom?" I ask, my voice quiet.

He turns to face me. "It's been good. She's exactly the same, like she just stepped back into her old life."

I swallow. I can tell by his tone that this bothers him for some reason. "And?" I ask, placing a hand on his.

He sighs. "And I'm not. Her getting committed was such a huge part of my life, but it's almost like she thinks she went to go run errands or something." He's quiet for a minute. "It makes me wonder if she even missed me."

Something cleaves in my chest at his words. "She loves you, Ash. She remained strong—for you. Not despite you. *For* you. So that when she was able to come back to you, she could show you what strength looked like—so she could protect you from the things she probably felt and saw."

He puts an arm around me and pulls me close, exhaling loudly. "Yeah. You're probably right."

"My mom is the same way," I add, whispering. "She stays strong in front of me, but growing up, I heard her crying alone in her room plenty of times."

He nods. "My father is an asshole, and I feel ashamed to be related to him."

I put my phone in my pocket, crossing my legs. "Hunter said the Greythorn name is old. Maybe there's someone else who can make you proud to be a Greythorn?"

He's quiet for a minute, eventually pointing to the park. "The mausoleum, Elias Greythorn. He was born in 1702, and he founded this town." He tugs me closer, and I relax against him.

"See? There you go." I look into the park. "That's where you were all drinking that first day—when you called out to me."

I remember that day so clearly. Having just moved to Greythorn—and I hadn't even met the guys yet. Still, they intrigued me even then.

He chuckles. "Yeah. Do you want to see it? I have a key."

Shivers work their way down my spine. "A key? To what?"

He shrugs. "His tomb."

I pull away. "I didn't realize they made keys for tombs."

He gives me a lopsided smile, and in the clear morning light, his eyes are the palest of blue.

"They don't normally. But nothing about Elias Greythorn was normal. He was very eclectic. He was a good guy, when not a lot of men back then were good guys."

Standing, he tugs me along after him. We enter the park, and today it's so much quieter than that first day. Walking toward the thickest part of the park, I gape when I see the large, stone structure come into view. It's not just a mausoleum—it's a small house.

Ash pulls a skeleton key from his pocket, walking to the door. "Wait," I hiss. "Is his...body...in there?"

Ash laughs—tipping his head back as the sound echoes against the trees. "No body. It was just a place he wanted his family to remember him. He's buried in the cemetery just outside of town."

He opens the tomb, and we step inside. It's just four walls with a stone seat built into one of them. There's a small window made of warped glass, and the gas lamp on the wall speaks of another time. Ash closes the door behind him, letting the silence permeate the space. It smells like damp grass, and because of the stone, it's at least ten degrees colder than outside.

"The weight of the Greythorn name is sometimes too heavy to bear," he explains, his voice frayed, uneven. His eyes find mine, the light from the window shining down on him. "I'm supposed to live up to this honored ancestor. I can't wait to leave it all behind. Find a place where no one knows about my father, or my mother, or the Kings."

I take a step toward him. "I wish you could see yourself the way I see you," I mumble, unzipping my jacket and shrugging it off, letting it fall to the floor.

His gaze is blazing now, his eyes two blue flames. "And how do you see me, Briar?"

I lean against the opposite wall, trying not to shiver. "Broken. Beautiful. Cunning. Loyal as fuck. Raunchy."

He laughs. "Raunchy?"

I smile. "Yeah. I mean, you do things to me that no one else dares to do."

Something unleashes from him then, because he walks forward, pressing his lips against mine. His body is hard under his clothes, and I groan as he places two hands on my breasts, squeezing as he moans. Then he drops them, reaching down and pulling my pants off in one frenzied movement. He lifts me up, and I wrap my legs around his waist as he pushes me against the cold, stone wall. Then, he unzips his pants.

I tilt my head back and gasp as he enters me, his head thick as it slides in with ease. He pushes into me, and I buck my hips against his, and then he stops moving as I ride him. He grips my ass, and I undulate my hips back and forth, arching my back as I get closer.

"Fuck," Ash whispers. "Look at how well you ride my cock, Briar." He grabs my chin and forces me to look—to see his wet shaft, so large, he practically hits bone when he's inside me fully...

I move against him, and he growls in response, his hands squeezing my flesh with need.

"I want to make you feel good," I whimper. "I want you, Ash."

He lets out a feral cry as I change my angle a bit, and he slams a hand against the stone near my head, breathing heavily. Watching him come undone like this, unraveling before my eyes as I ride him...

Watching him watch us—his eyes looking down, the way his chest rises and falls unevenly, like he's trying to catch his breath—sets me off. His eyes flick up to my face and he watches me with furrowed concentration, with animalistic need. My climax starts slowly, and I feel myself grip him with every wave, feeling every muscle release inside me in a cacophony of pleasure. I soak his shirt, clawing my fingers down his arms, a whimpering mess.

Feeling me come around him makes him let out a frenzied desperate cry, but he doesn't move as his cock pulses into me—he releases inside of me, his expression intense with disbelief, like he didn't expect to come like that. His shaft rises and falls, his hands gripping me firmly, and then he sags against me as the last of it leaves his body.

"I've fucked a lot of women," he starts, and I bark out a surprised laugh. "But your pussy feels the best. I'll never be able to fuck someone else now."

I snort. "I'm sure you'd be able to find someone—"

His hand comes to my face, and he kisses me roughly, his tongue needy and firm. When he pulls back and lowers me to the ground, he growls as he presses himself against me.

"I'm not joking. I'll never get my fill, and I don't want to be with anyone else."

His words cause my throat to tighten up, my chest to ache. "I feel the same way," I whisper.

"I don't fucking care about my friends, either. I just need you—however I can have you."

I nod and grip the fabric of his shirt. "I'm yours," I answer.

This might be the best thing that ever happened to either of us.

28

ASH

I walk Briar home, and then I head toward my house a couple miles away. I think about what she said—about my mom hiding the horrors of the hospital from me. I think of the nights we've spent together since she's been home— the meals she's cooked, the floors she's mopped—and I wonder if she goes into her room and cries, like Briar's mom. My heart breaks a little bit just thinking about it.

As I walk through the door, the heaviness in my chest intensifies when I see her sitting at the dining room table. There are two plates.

She made me breakfast.

"Hi," I say, closing the door behind me.

"Hey, sweetie. Where have you been?" It's not accusatory. She knows I'm eighteen, and she's not exactly going to enforce the same rules my father did. If I was one minute past curfew, he'd beat me up.

"I just went on a walk," I explain, sitting down and shoveling eggs and toast in my mouth. I didn't realize how hungry I was. "I needed to clear my head."

About you. About Briar. About Dad. About...everything.

"I see. Well, I put your clean clothes on your bed, and I ordered that shampoo you like, so that should be here tomorrow—"

"Mom." I place my fork down on the table a little too loudly. "You don't have to pretend to be holding it all together. I know you probably had to deal with a lot being in there, and I don't expect you to waltz back here like nothing happened," I add, my voice rough and gritty.

She frowns, and the lines in her forehead deepen. Her pale blue eyes—*my eyes*—soften around the corners. "I didn't expect that, either. I thought I'd be a mess. And it's only been a couple of weeks, but I feel...okay, Ash."

Her words caress some locked-up part inside of me, and I swallow. "I just don't want you to put on a brave face for my benefit, that's all."

She reaches out and takes my hand. "I'm not. I promise. I have my baggage from that place, but do you know what I hoped for, every single day?"

I shake my head. "What?"

"To see you," she answers softly. "To be a part of your life again. I didn't care about anything else. So when I was released, it felt as though my prayers had been answered. Of course there are things I have to deal with, but overall, I feel lucky, grateful, and blessed to be here with you."

I swallow. "I'm glad you're here."

"Me too, sweetie. Me too."

We go back to eating, and I can't help but feel slightly lighter than before.

"I hope he rots in his cell," I add, and I swear I see a hint of a smile on my mother's red lips.

❧ 29 ❧

BRIAR

The atmosphere at Ravenwood Academy the morning of Halloween is frenzied—and excited. For the last two weeks, Scarlett and Jack have become the plus two to our group. In fact, their seamless integration is so subtle that I don't notice the aftereffects for a few days. Slowly but surely, people begin to smile at us. Instead of fear in their eyes, we are met with a little trepidation, but also a little curiosity. Since Micah—and then me—no one has penetrated the reign of the Kings.

So on the morning of Halloween, a few people take a chance and sit with us in the center of the quad, and no one says anything—not even Ash, who looks slightly suspicious. I know he means well, and he does an excellent job of *not* glaring at people, but it's going to be an adjustment for all of them. Over the course of the day, most of the students slowly walk by and study us. The dictatorship seems to be crumbling with each passing day.

At lunch, a few freshman girls ask me about the Halloween Carnival tonight. There are flyers all over campus, but I think they want to test the waters to see if the rumors are true. I give them all warm smiles and hand them a few free ride passes. They walk away giggling, and I can't help but smile because it solidifies what I think I've known for a few weeks: the reputation of the Kings is unfounded, and people might finally be starting to realize it.

Costumes aren't allowed at Ravenwood Academy, but I manage to find a badass Edward Scissorhands costume for later, complete with long, silver nails (I opted out of actual scissors for practical reasons), and a leather ensemble. I can't wait to wear it. The guys opted out of wearing costumes, and I try not to laugh at their lack of Halloween spirit. But then I remember, not everyone is obsessed with All Hallows Eve like me.

Scarlett and Jack opt to go as the Wicked Witch of the West and the Wizard of Oz. After school, Scarlett, Jack, Hunter, and I all head back to the house to get ready for the carnival. My nerves are shot the minute we leave school, because I know tonight might be the night we catch Cam. I've made a conscious effort not to think about it too much, because every time I do, I want to back out.

But then I remember that I have four guys who have vowed to protect me, my mom and Andrew, Scarlett and Jack, and the security of twenty police officers. Tickets are sold out, and Andrew suspects the vast majority of Greythorn residents will be present. Plus, the authorities have been trained for this. They have regimented plans, foolproof strategies. This may have been our idea, but they'll take over from here. If Cam shows up, they will find him.

"This is gorgeous," Scarlett croons, running a hand down the black leather bodice of my costume.

"Thanks," I muse, looking at myself in the large mirror in my bedroom.

"It enhances certain aspects," Jack muses, joking.

He's referring to the low-cut neckline. He's donning a dark green tuxedo, and his hair is slicked back.

As Scarlett and I fix our hair in my mirror, I can't help but smile. Even though parts of tonight might be daunting —and I have no idea how it will all go down, so the unpredictability is nauseating—at least Scarlett and Jack don't hate me anymore.

Scarlett's black cloak and green makeup is exquisite. She's added black lipstick and thick, black eyelashes, while also accentuating her eyebrow arches. Just as we pull our shoes on, Hunter walks in, taking in all our costumes. Jack and Scarlett make a great pair, and Scarlett picks up her broom, grinning. I see Hunter try to hide his smile as he turns to me.

I have on a leather bodice and matching leather pants with multiple belts around my middle, and black combat boots. I teased my hair so that it's wild, and I hold my hands out, showing him my long nails.

"Damn, Ravenwood," Jack taunts. "Do you hate Halloween or something?" He's referring to the lack of costume.

"It's not really my thing," he muses, giving us all a small smile. He bends down to kiss me, and Scarlett clears her throat. She's been a little more reserved with the guys—especially Samson. I don't blame her. Everyone is getting used to things being different, getting used to each other. We all head downstairs.

My mom takes a million pictures. Andrew and my mom are Dumbledore and Hagrid from Harry Potter—my mom being Hagrid. Her fake beard is endearing, and I can't help but snort when they kiss each other and their beards get tangled. Wiping my sweaty palms on my dress, I feel my pulse tick up with each passing minute.

We'd discussed what would happen at the carnival, how five officers in disguise would take a place on each corner of the town square. The nine of us—including my parents—are supposed to go about their nights as usual.

I just have to hope beyond belief that one, he comes, and two, the authorities are able to arrest him.

"Okay, how is everyone getting there?" Andrew muses.

"I can take Jack," Scarlett volunteers.

"I'll ride with Briar and our parents," Hunter adds.

"That works!" My mom grabs her purse, and then she, Andrew, and my friends file outside.

Hunter turns to face me. "Ready?"

I swallow.

Am I ready?

To what—capture my rapist? Hope he walks into the trap we set? A lot is riding on tonight. If he doesn't come, or if he gets away again...

I shake my head. "Why don't I drive separately? I... I need a bit of space."

His brows furrow. "Briar, I really don't think you should be alone tonight." Pulling me into him, he kisses my brow. "Let me wait with you," he suggests.

I give him a long, slow kiss—my hands getting tangled in his thick, dark hair as I run my fingers through it. Pulling away, I touch my lips.

"I think I'm going to text Sonya. I just need...reassurance, I guess." He looks at me skeptically, so I offer him an olive branch. "What if we walk out together? I'll look my car doors, call Sonya, and meet you there in five?"

He watches me for a second, his pupils darkening. "Are you sure?"

I smile. "You go with the bearded lizards," I joke, referring to my mom and Andrew. "I'll be right behind you."

He nods. "Alright. If you insist. I'll let our parents know."

I grab my purse as we walk out together. I see my mom and Andrew waiting in Andrew's Lexus. Hunter leans down, giving me a kiss on the forehead.

"I'll see you in a few," he murmurs.

I wave to them and walk to the Subaru. They watch me get in, and once it's locked, they give me a thumbs up and drive away. I lean against my seat, taking a few deep breaths.

I'm fine. Everything is fine. I am safe.

I pick my phone up and text Sonya, and while I don't go into explicit detail, I just tell her that I'm nervous with Cam having escaped prison. I leave out the part about him swarming us—*me*—like a shark.

But I fought back last time, and I will fight back this time—by beating him at his own game. By outsmarting him. By ensuring I'm never in that position again. We have so many people watching out for him tonight, and he has no idea. If we'd had someone watching for him at homecoming...

I push the thought away.

He was so close—and yet, we weren't prepared.

But we *are* prepared tonight.

Sonya's text comes through just as I'm about to start the car, so I relax against my seat and read it.

Evaluate your surroundings. Listen to your gut. Apply common sense. These three things will almost never fail you. Be smart, but you also need to live your life. The chances of Cam being anywhere near Greythorn are so small. Enjoy your night, and Happy Halloween!

I try to find comfort in her words, but I can't—not right now. Because he is in Greythorn—and I've seen him.

And now it's time to take him down—once and for all.

I toss my phone into my purse, and then I quickly pull the mirror down to check that my black eyeliner hasn't smudged. I stare at my reflection. My face is calm. Serene. Despite the upheaval, despite my past coming back and haunting me, I know that whatever I'm doing right now is good for my soul.

Hunter, Ash, Ledger, and Samson...they are my saviors.

They are good for my soul.

Smiling, I close the mirror, and my eyes catch on the movement in front of my car. My stomach bottoms out, and my veins pulse painfully beneath my flesh.

I am frozen—paralyzed. And my heart pounds against my ribs painfully.

"Hello, Briar," Cam says loudly enough for me to hear. He's in a white shirt and jeans, and I can see the thick, dark scar running down his neck from here. I frantically fish for my keys, my phone, *anything*—but he growls and throws my door open, grabbing me underneath my arms and dragging me out of my car.

My door. I forgot to lock my door, like I promised Hunter.

My pulse is rushing in my ears. I kick against the driveway, screaming, but he's too strong, too big. "Open the door," he commands, throwing my purse at me as I scramble away from him. We're a few feet from the front door. "And turn the camera off."

He must know about the smart camera, then.

"Fuck you," I hiss, grabbing my purse and hunting for my phone.

"You looking for this?" he asks, smirking. He has my phone in his hand, and he crouches down to where I'm sitting. "Don't even think of running away, Briar. Or calling one of your boyfriends. Turn. The. Camera. Off," he growls, handing my phone to me.

My lips tremble slightly as I unlock my phone, and he watches my every move as I open the app and disable everything.

"Good girl." In one swift motion, he yanks my phone out of my hands—my last lifeline—and throws it against the driveway.

It shatters, and my heart sinks.

Before I can react, scream, anything—he grabs my hair and drags me to the door. With a foot on my stomach, he empties my purse and finds the keys, unlocking the door. I try not to panic, instead pounding against his thick calf. It's no use. He's like a stone statue. I scream one more time before he drags me inside and slams the door shut.

Picking me up, he throws me against the foyer wall, my face smashed against the drywall. He comes up behind me, and his breath is hot and sticky on my exposed neck. I feel hands roam to my ass, gripping it roughly as he sniffs my hair.

Just like ten months ago.

Just like before.

No.

"I think we need to have a little chat," he says, fisting my hair and dragging me away.

30

Samson

I keep waiting for her green Subaru to drive into the parking lot, and every SUV that could be hers sends me craning my neck over the fence I'm standing by. When I met up with Hunter, he told me she would be here in a minute, and our float ride is in less than an hour. I check my watch—it's been twenty-six minutes. No sign of Cam, but also no sign of Briar.

Pulling out my phone, I text her, and the message stays on delivered—no read receipt like usual I glance around at the carnival goers, ensuring none of them look like the tall, muscular guy I saw in the grocery store a few weeks ago...

My uncle is working kitchen setup outside his restaurant on the perimeter of the square. I see Ledger with his brother, who came in from Boston to see his friends play. I know they plan to start soon. Hunter is by the raffle, encouraging everyone to enter—but I see the way his eyes scan the crowd. Aubrey and Andrew are sitting near the food, enjoying funnel cakes—though Aubrey checks her phone nearly as much as I do. Ash is talking to the furniture rental company, and Scarlett and Jack are on the other ride—a small rollercoaster—completely oblivious to the fact that Briar's rapist could be here.

Could be.

I swallow and push my glasses up. What if he doesn't show up? What if he sees through our plan? There are a few officers stationed at other points in Greythorn, in disguise. I just have to hope that one of them finds him if he chooses not to come here.

I check my phone again a few minutes later, and it's still on delivered.

Fuck.

It's been thirty minutes, and she's barely a five-minute drive away.

She should be here by now.

I jog over to Ash, but he tells me he hasn't seen Briar. I find Hunter next.

"Hey man, where is she? We have to be on the float in like ten minutes."

Hunter glances down at his phone. "She's not answering my texts."

I fidget with the hem on my shirt, trying not to think of the reason she could be late. "Try calling her. Maybe she got distracted—"

He already has the phone up to his ear. "Fuck," he hisses, looking at his screen. "It went straight to voicemail. Maybe she's talking to her therapist." He tries again and lets out an exasperated breath. "Hold on, Aubrey has her location on her phone. Let's go check where she is."

We head over to where Aubrey and Andrew are laughing with beards full of powdered sugar, and Hunter asks her if he can check on Briar. A hint of worry passes over her face.

"It says 'Location Not Available.' Looking at me, her lips thin. "Maybe she turned her phone off, but I think one of us should check on her."

I nod. "I'm on it, Mrs. Monroe." We walk back to the front gate.

Hunter shrugs. "Maybe she lost track of time talking to Sonya?"

I chew on the inside of my cheek. "I don't buy it. She'd be talking on her phone, and she would've seen our notifications. It seems like her phone is off." I look up at him. "She was in her car, right?"

His brows knit together. "Yeah. She said she would be leaving in a minute."

I grab my phone and text Ledger and Ash. "Something's not right. Come on, let's go."

Hunter gestures to Aubrey, who jumps up and follows us, and he gives them the key to his car.

"You guys drive separately. I'm parked two blocks that way," he says, gesturing toward the park. "I'll ride with the guys."

By the time Hunter and I make it to my car in the lot, Ledger and Ash are right behind us.

We all share a look—the same dark, agitated expressions.

Please be okay.
She has to be okay.

❧ 31 ❧

BRIAR

My screams are muffled as he ties me up to one of the dining room chairs. He's so cliché—using duct tape. I would laugh if I could, but he placed a piece of tape over my mouth first thing. The motherfucker didn't enjoy me hurling insults at him as he carried me over his shoulder. I *did* manage to bite a chunk of flesh off his arm, and his rage and subsequent bellow caused him to throw me against the hard floor. I'm pretty sure he broke one of my ribs, but I'm trying not to think about it.

"Your whore mother thinks she leveled up, huh?" he asks, his voice slightly slurred as he takes in the mansion. *Ahh, nothing like a psycho rapist...especially a* drunk *psycho rapist.* I glare at him as he circles me. "My, my, Briar," he purrs. "You've really filled out this year." His eyes flick to my chest.

My heart clenches when I think of him—of all the guys. If something happens to me...*to them*...

"You were so fucking easy to find," he adds, smiling as he swings his arms. "And it was simple enough to get here by car from California. Of course, I knew what to watch out for, being a cop once upon a time. But I'm honestly surprised you didn't try to hide your whereabouts a bit better," he muses.

I want to scream, but my throat is already raw.

I kick my feet out at him, my tongue tasting the bitter glue of the duct tape, and he snarls. "You've turned into such a feisty bitch, pretty girl."

That nickname makes me want to vomit. The whole night begins to flash through my mind, and even though Sonya and I have worked through it, seeing Cam here, hearing those words...

I remember the fear of his body overpowering mine. The pain, the violation of the rape. And then the shock at having stabbed him. The cold when I ran out the back door. The way the mud and twigs caught on my bare feet, how my feet were cut up for weeks. I remember the panic rising in my throat like bile, making me spit every few steps, making me feel feral and wild, like an animal. I remember my dress, plastered to my body from the wet, windy mist. I remember the anger.

The soul-wrenching, burning *anger*.

At what he'd done.

I'd trusted him.

And he'd betrayed me in the worst way possible.

I dig my nails into my palm, my tears sliding down my cheeks as Cam paces the dining room.

"I'm going to make sure that if and when I'm caught, at

least the smug, little cunt who ruined my life will be dead. What do you think, pretty girl?"

I begin to shake, my eyelashes wet against my face. *I am strong. I survived. I fought back—I really fucking fought back.*

I did everything right.

He's in the wrong.

I need to fight back.

Narrowing my eyes at him, I force my body to still. Being scared won't do me any good right now. I refuse to let him hurt me again. I refuse to become another statistic. I did not go through what I went through just to have my rapist kill me after everything. This is not going to be the end of my story.

Cam walks over and stares down at me. My chest is rising and falling, and I will myself to be calm. *Think, Briar. Think.* His nostrils flare as I narrow my eyes and give him a hateful expression. *I will win this fight.*

Reaching down, he rips the tape off my mouth, and my eyes water as I bare my teeth at him.

"What do you want, Cam? You want me dead? What does that accomplish? I don't want to die, and you don't want to go to jail for life."

He chuckles, running a hand over his lips. "So? I didn't want to go to jail for thirteen years. Sometimes life's not fair."

I start to respond, but then he pulls a knife out of his waistband. My whole body runs cold, and I feel a trickle of sweat run down my back underneath the leather bodysuit. He tips my chin up with the point of the knife, and I glare at him.

I won't die this way.

"I'm going to kill you the same way you almost killed me. Nothing you say will change my mind, pretty girl. I didn't formulate an escape plan and put three of my friends in danger for nothing. I didn't drive across the country for *nothing*," he spits, digging the point into my skin. I feel the blood begin to pool in that spot, and I hold back a whimper. "I've already accepted my fate, Briar. Have you?"

Before I can say anything, he drops to his knees.

No.

Grinning maniacally, he pulls my pants off, sitting back on his haunches as he stares at the bareness between my legs.

I'm not wearing undies.

It was supposed to be a treat for Samson.

"You fucking slut," he snarls, running the smooth back of the knife along my leg. "Did you do this for me? You think I didn't know you were hoping to turn me in tonight? You think I didn't know the fucking posters with your face were for me? Or the way you stayed behind tonight? Can't you admit you did it all for me?"

No.

Never.

But...

This is my chance.

My chance to get revenge.

My chance to take him down.

Play this right, Briar.

"Yes," I say softly, faking a sob. "Yes. Okay? Are you happy now?"

He stills, and his eyes find mine, searching for the lie.

But I let my lip wobble slightly, shrugging as much as I can all tied up.

"I didn't think you'd attack me like this," I add. "Not after what happened. I knew you escaped for me, Cam. I hoped you would. I made a mistake that night," I finish, sobbing. "I was young and confused. I had such a crush on you—" His eyebrows shoot up, and I continue, feigning shyness. "I haven't been the same since everything happened."

"I don't believe you," he muses, taking the hilt of the knife and caressing the inside of my thigh, getting closer to... "If you wanted me to badly, why did I see all four of your worthless boyfriends fucking you at once?"

Squeezing my eyes shut, I breathe heavily, the bile beginning to creep up my esophagus.

My god, he saw everything.

I shake my head back and forth violently, trying to clear my mind of the idea that Cam was watching—that he was there. That he saw everything. It makes me gag, and Cam chuckles.

"Oh, you didn't know I saw you guys up there in the woods? I was so close at one point, I could've touched you." He clucks his tongue. "I almost killed you all then and there. I was so angry, Briar. So angry that you would so willingly spread your legs for them and not for me. But it would've been too obvious. Plus, I don't care enough about those pricks to kill them. Only you. I needed you alone, so I could finish what I started."

Snapping my eyes open, I sob again. "I'm sorry, okay? I thought... I thought they could be like you. I didn't know what else to do. You awakened something in me that night, Cam."

Believe me.

Believe me.

"They seem to really like you," he starts, placing the dull hilt against my opening. *No.* "They seem to love fucking you," he growls. "Just like I did."

Panic floods me, but I get a grip on it before it takes over.

Swallowing thickly, I nod. "You're right. I can't deny that what you're doing feels good," I groan, bucking my hips once. "I was so young before. But now? I've fucked most of the senior class just trying to get over you."

He gives me a monstrous smile. "Oh, really?"

He's buying it. Keep going.

I grin. "Of course." I look down, furrowing my brows. "I still don't understand why you attacked me, though. Couldn't you tell that I was waiting for you?"

Something moves behind his eyes—and he gives me a lecherous smile. "I know you so well, baby. You fucking whore."

No, you don't.

I give him a small smile. "Knife play is one of my kinks. I like it dirty—bloody. Just like that night. Keep going," I moan.

His eyes flash with something that makes me want to hide under my bed forever. But I can't—I have to play this *just right.*

"You're such a slut," he grunts, scooting closer. Swirling the knife around my opening, I close my mouth to keep from screaming—from roaring with fury.

I throw my head back in an exaggerated show, spreading my legs slightly so he has better access. I swallow the vomit working its way up my throat.

"Keep going then," I demand, biting my lower lip.

Keep going—a challenge.

Cam unbuckles his belt, and it takes every ounce of resolve not to head butt him—not to scream and claw my way out of this. But I don't know what else to do. I have to work him into a frenzy, and then I have to attack.

I look away as he pulls his cock out, feigning arousal as I squeeze my eyes shut. Thrusting upwards, I moan again, and this time, he lets out a low groan. I hear him spit into his hand and begin to stroke himself.

"I need better access," I whine, snapping my eyes open. "Untie my feet. Please." He hesitates, but I bite my lower lip again. "I want my legs over your shoulder."

He growls as he tears at the tape, but it doesn't budge.

"Spread your legs," he commands.

"What?"

"Your legs. Open your knees and the tape will tear with enough force from all sides."

I do as I'm told, and then Cam slams a hand down, effectively breaking through the layers of tape.

Interesting.

"The couch," I mumble. "You can keep my hands tied. I want them above my head."

He mumbles something, but he's not really paying attention—he's jacking himself off. In one swift movement, he picks me up and carries me to the couch in the living room across the hallway, and as my body hits the cushions, I cry out—faking it.

Even with a plan to murder me, even with all the power, he's still so, *so* stupid. He has no idea that with each request, I'm grabbing my power back.

"Yes," I whimper, spreading myself before him. I move

AMANDA RICHARDSON

my hands above my head as he lowers himself on top of me.

I can't breathe...

Gasping, I feel him trying to maneuver into me. While he's distracted, I rear my tied hands back farther, spreading them as wide as I can against the plastic.

One chance.

I have one chance.

I close my eyes and pray to whoever will listen that this works.

I have the upper hand.

I win this war.

In one fell swoop, I force my joined hands downward as hard as I can, and the tape breaks against Cam's skull before he realizes what's happening. I slam a knee into his groin, and we both roll off the couch. I scramble up and run for the knife in the other room.

"Briar!"

I twist just in time to see Hunter, Ash, Ledger, and Samson running toward me, and Cam coming from the other room.

"Watch out!" I scream, and instead of coming for me, Cam rushes to the guys.

Idiot.

Ash roars and unleashes upon him, punching him in the face with such force that I hear a crack. Cam stumbles backwards, and I slide the knife over to them.

Samson looks down at it, and then his eyes meet mine as he slides it back with his foot.

"All you, little lamb."

"Fucking finish what you started," Ledger growls.

Hunter nods, looking down at the knife and then at me. "Do it."

"If you don't, I fucking will," Ash snarls.

"Briar—please—" Cam rasps, stumbling as he tries to get up. He begins to crawl to me—his face red and pained, his nose pouring blood.

Cracking a smile, I cock my head as I rush over.

And I stab him in the chest—once.

Twice.

Three times.

When he falls onto his stomach, prone and unmoving, I wait until I don't feel a pulse before standing. The knife clatters to the ground.

He didn't finish what he started.

I did.

32

BRIAR

The world tilts a bit, and Samson rushes over just as I faint. When I come to, the police are checking Cam's pulse, and my mom and Andrew are speaking to them. Someone must've pulled my pants back on because they're loose and around my waist. I tie them tighter, sitting up as a couple of cops notice my movements. My mom rushes over to me.

"Briar, oh honey," my mom sobs, pulling me close. We hold each other, swaying in place, for what feels like forever. Andrew puts a warm hand on my shoulder. I relax fully for the first time in weeks. "I'm so sorry," she whispers, hugging me tightly.

"It's okay. I'm okay," I murmur.

I'm not sure if I'm trying to reassure her, or myself.

"Ms. Monroe? We have a few questions for you," the sheriff asks, his face apologetic.

"Of course."

I am hounded with questions, and I answer them all truthfully.

He attacked me.

I stabbed him.

The guys walked in just before I killed him.

It was self-defense.

After a few minutes of additional questioning, they're satisfied with my answers, and then they move onto the guys as I sag against my mom on the couch. I don't look as they wheel Cam away.

"Ma'am," one of the officers says, walking over to me with a piece of paper. "We still need you to answer some additional questions, but you can come into the station tomorrow."

I nod. "Sure. Whatever I can do to put this behind me," I respond.

Once and for all...

He nods and gives me a sympathetic look. "Get some rest tonight." He walks away slowly, looking down at his phone.

"Wait!" I cry. He turns, eyebrows raised. "He said three friends helped him escape in California. You might want to make sure the Marin City police department knows."

He gives me a small smile. "Do you have any names, or any other information you could give me?"

I shrug. "No. He just said three people helped him escape San Quentin."

He nods solemnly. "Thank you. I'll put in a call to his old station tonight."

And then he's gone, leaving me alone with my family—and the guys.

"Someone should tell Scarlett and Jack," I murmur.

"I'm on it," Andrew offers, grabbing his phone and texting them.

I turn to my mom. "I think I'm going to go upstairs and clean up," I say quietly, the shock still numbing me. "I —I have his blood all over me," I say quietly, looking down at myself.

"Do whatever you need to do. How about I make you some tea?" Her eyes flick to the guys briefly.

I nod. "Sure. Thanks, mom."

She gives me a small smile, kissing my forehead. "Just come down whenever you're ready." Her and Andrew walk to the kitchen, leaving the five of us alone.

I turn to face the guys, and none of them say anything. For whatever reason, I feel the need to explain.

"I didn't realize he would be—"

"Briar," Hunter commands, crossing his arms. "There is no excuse for what he did."

"I know, but I should have—"

"What? Anticipated that your rapist would be waiting for the second you were all alone?" Ash adds, his voice tight.

I shrug. "My therapist taught me how to evaluate if a situation is safe. Evaluate your surroundings. Listen to your gut. Apply common sense."

Ledger shakes his head and looks away, and Samson walks up to me, taking my hands.

"Those are great parameters to abide by, but this was... different. Okay? Nothing you could've done would've stopped him. If it wasn't tonight, it would've been in a week, or a month, or..." he trails off, closing his eyes briefly as his jaw ticks. "He would've slipped past your self-imposed guards somehow. I don't think your therapist accounted for a situation like this."

"He's right," Ledger says, rubbing his mouth with his hand. "And I'm not discrediting her wisdom, because it's good advice. But someone you're close to who rapes you? And the same guy who attacks you when you're alone? What could you have done differently?"

They're right, of course.

The three rules that Sonya taught me will only get me so far. People know how to slip past the warning signs—people can follow all the rules until it really matters. For example, getting close to your girlfriend's daughter so that she trusts you. Or waiting until she's alone to attack her with a knife. The three rules couldn't have saved me in either scenario.

They couldn't save me, but I saved myself both times.

And that must count for something.

Swallowing, I look down. "He saw us. He was there—the night we were camping."

Hunter's eyebrows come together, and I see him ball his fists. Ash swears and turns away, kicking something invisible. Ledger just crosses his arms and frowns, and Samson is schooling his face into neutrality—but I see the way his jaw ticks.

"I swear to God, if that motherfucker wasn't already dead," Ash hisses, placing a hand over his mouth.

"He's dead, man," Ledger says quietly. "He lost. We won."

Hunter is quiet as he fidgets with his jaw, his feet tapping on the floor. "I think I can speak for all of us when I say, I'm glad you're safe, Briar."

I swallow and I glance at each of them. "I was sure he

was going to kill me. I just want it all behind me." My voice catches on the last word, and I look down at my hands, which are still stained with blood. I clench my fists at my sides as I shake my head. "I thought it would be easy —seeing him again. *Facing* him again. But it was just as hard as the first time."

Ash takes my hand. "Come on. Let's get you cleaned up." I pull away, opening my mouth to protest, but he interrupts me. "We couldn't help you. We got here too late. So let us at least take care of you now."

"Ash—"

"He's right," Hunter ponders with a scowl. "You fought back, and that's fucking badass."

I give him a grateful smile.

"Briar, would you rather be by yourself?" Samson asks, glancing at Ash with annoyance.

I love that they look out for me—that each of them is in tune with a specific part of me, that they can each figure me out in their own ways.

I shake my head. "No. I don't want to be alone."

Ledger walks to the stairs. "Come on. Let's get you cleaned up."

I follow him upstairs—the other guys close behind.

❧ 33 ❧

HUNTER

I kneel on the floor of Briar's bathroom, helping her step out of her shoes. Ash pulls her dress over her head, Samson starts the bath, and Ledger stands next to her, wiping her arms with a washcloth—ensuring all the dried blood is gone. It hits me then—how alike these things are with relation to her.

Me at her feet, worshipping her strength, her soul.

Ash helping her out of her clothes, worshipping her body.

Ledger cleaning her up, worshipping her physical health, ensuring she's fully taken care of in that department.

And Samson pouring bath salts into her bath, worshipping her mental health—checking in, going slow, thinking about what will make her comfortable.

I swallow as I stand, and Ash helps her into the bath.

None of us crosses that boundary. I think we're all under the assumption that she doesn't want to be touched—doesn't want *that* aspect of her relationship with us right now. Which is why her next words stun me—stun *us*.

"Which one of you is getting in with me?" she purrs, bringing her knees up and resting her cheek on them.

"Briar, maybe you should just sleep tonight," Samson offers, and a very, very small part of me wants to tell him to shut his fucking mouth.

But the bigger part of me agrees.

"No," she whispers. "I'm done being afraid," she starts, sniffing. "He ruined my junior year in California. Ruined men for me for a long time. Ruined homecoming, and Halloween..." Swallowing, she looks down at the water as her hands trail through the soapy liquid. "I feel good when I'm with you guys, and right now, I really, *really* need to feel good. I want to salvage the night. I want to remember being with you. Not—not him."

We all watch her for a beat. "I'll get in with you," Ash offers quickly, already removing his clothes.

Samson snorts, leaning against the door, and I sit on the counter, trying not to smile. Ledger leans against the glass of the shower. We all share a look, but they don't ask us to leave.

Ash climbs in behind her, and Samson's gaze heats when he notices Ash's erection. He clears his throat.

"I can go—" I offer, pointing to the door with my thumb.

Briar looks over her shoulder at me. "Stay."

A command—not a question.

Our Queen.

Oh, how the tables have turned—and I wouldn't have it any other way.

She leans back against Ash, who cups her breasts in his large hands. I shift, wondering if I should acknowledge my hard on, or ignore it like Ledger and Samson seem to be doing.

Ash's hands trail down her stomach, water pooling in her belly button. She moans, closing her eyes as she arches her back slightly. Suddenly, the physical need to be inside her is all consuming. Ash groans, and his hand finds its way between her legs. I crane my neck to see, but it's covered with cloudy water. Still, my cock pulses inside my pants when I see Ash's fingers working her.

"Does murder make you wet, little lamb?" Ash croons, bucking his hips against hers.

"No. You do." Opening her eyes, she meets our gazes. "All of you," she clarifies.

It makes me happy to see her enjoying this after tonight's nightmare. I can't wait to make her feel good— can't wait for each of us to make her feel good.

If she said jump, we would jump.

I pull my shirt over my head, and Samson and Ledger do the same. Stepping out of my pants, I stroke my throbbing shaft. Ash's tempo gets quicker, and Briar writhes against him—her nipples pink and hard. I let out a shaky breath at the sight of her perfect tits bouncing.

"You're so fucking beautiful," Ash whispers. He removes his hand from between her legs maneuvers his cock there instead. Her sharp inhale lets me know he's inside her, and he moves underneath her, gripping her side as he thrusts deep. The water threatens to spill over the edge of the clawfoot tub.

"Oh, God," she whimpers, squeezing her eyes shut.

I wasn't sure if I'd enjoy seeing someone else fuck her. Last time we all did this, I was behind her, fucking her ass. But this is *hot*. Especially as I glance at my other friends, who have the same heated expressions—their cocks in their hands.

"Ash," she groans. "Harder. I want you to fuck the thought of him out of me."

"Fuck," Ash rasps. "Happy to oblige, my Queen."

And then he pushes her forward onto her knees, slamming into her from behind.

She screams, and the sound reverberates around the small room.

"Yes, Ash, yes," she cries. "Deeper. I want to feel you everywhere."

"Holy shit," I utter, my knees going weak. I hold on to the counter, steadying myself. *This is so fucking hot.* Everything about her—every single imperfection, every single personality trait—is perfect. *This* is perfect.

"Come for me, Briar," Ash growls.

She looks over her shoulder at me furtively before flicking her eyes to Ledger and Samson. Arching her back and gripping the edge of the tub, she pants.

"Oh, fuck," she says quietly, and I see the crescendo of muscles contracting from her core to the rest of her limbs. Shaking, she bellows as she explodes, twitching with every wave, her eyes fluttering closed.

"Holy shit," Ash whispers. "I'm coming."

He fills her, grunting and grabbing the flesh of her ass, pulling her onto his cock forcefully as the last of it leaves him. They both collapse against the edge of the tub.

I slow my hand. "Briar, go to your bedroom."

She obeys, and the other guys follow me.

"I want you," she starts, looking at me. Then her eyes find Ledger. "And you."

I'm not sure when it's agreed that I'll take her pussy this time, but soon she's climbing on top of me. I look over at Ash, who is on his knees before Samson.

Fuck, if I weren't straight...

"Relax, Briar," Ledger growls as she lowers herself onto me. He has a bottle of lube in his hands.

"Fuck," I hiss. "You're so fucking wet."

"You're welcome," Ash says, and we all laugh.

Briar closes her eyes as she takes me in fully, and we both hiss.

"Open your eyes," I say. When she looks at me, straight fire shines through her pupils. Her chest is flushed, and she shudders when I run my finger down her abdomen.

"Please," she pleads, her eyes hooded as she looks back at Ledger.

He spreads her ass, and her eyes widen a bit as he slowly moves inside her. Like before, I feel his cock slide against mine through her thin wall.

Holy fucking shit.

She reaches down and plays with herself, and I throw my head back at the double sensations. We both cry out as I quickly drive into her, more stars exploding before me. As she moves on top of me, her pussy milking my cock with each movement, I look over at Samson just as he groans and spills into Ash's mouth.

Fuck.

Fuck.

My climax builds quicker than I expected, my shaft

beginning to throb inside her. She's close, too, because she grabs my hand and moves it to her clit. I swirl my thumb around, using her wetness or Ash's cum or my pre-cum—whatever it is—and that thought pushes me over the edge.

"Holy fuck." My voice breaks. Her breathing is labored, and her eyes don't leave mine. Her warm pussy, swollen with need, contracts tightly around me, setting me off at the same time. Waves of pleasure shoot through me as I watch her come on top of me. My eyes stay locked on her as I pour into her.

She is mine—and I am hers. *We* are hers.

"I'm coming," Ledger says, hissing as he jerks. Briar's mouth pops open, and her hand goes back around to him. Biting her lower lip, she turns back to me, smiling.

Samson is cleaning himself up when Ledger pulls out, and Briar climbs off me.

"I'll never get enough of you," Ledger murmurs into her ear while cleaning her up.

"Thank you," she replies, looking at each of us with such openness, such vulnerability, that something in my chest cleaves in half. "All of you."

"Get some sleep," Ash says, pulling his clothes back on. Turning to Samson and Ledger, he gestures to the door. "Come on. She needs sleep now."

They each give her a kiss, and soon it's just the two of us.

She changes into pajamas, using the restroom and washing her face. I sit on the edge of her bed and rub my temples, waiting to tuck her in. She climbs into the flannel sheets, sighing contentedly.

She's content—*we* did that.

Even though we weren't there until the very end—a

fact that bothers me to no end—we were able to help her in other ways. The oath we took doesn't change just because the man we vowed to protect her from is now dead.

I don't think any of us wants to ever give her up.

"Stay with me?" she asks, closing her eyes.

My dad will know—as will Aubrey. They could open her door and see us when they get home. But fuck it. She comes first. I'll explain everything tomorrow.

Pulling my underwear on, I climb in behind her.

"Don't leave, okay?" she asks, her voice already slurred with exhaustion.

"Okay," I whisper. "And Briar?"

"Hmm?"

"I love you." I don't know what else to say. Only those three words can adequately summarize how I feel about her.

"I love you, too," she murmurs.

She has no idea how much I worship her, how I would do anything for her. Getting to her tonight... I would've burned the world to the ground to save her.

But she saved herself.

A true Queen.

34

LEDGER

Six Weeks Later

I wait for Briar to answer the door, jogging in place so that the frosty, December morning doesn't freeze up my muscles. When the door swings open, she grins at me.

"You look cute in your hat and scarf," she croons, tying her own scarf around her neck and pulling on a beanie.

I smirk. "I could say the same thing, little lamb." I tickle her playfully.

We start gradually—the cold causing us to go slower than normal until we're fully warmed up, about a mile in.

She doesn't fall behind, doesn't ask to stop, the entire six miles. When we nearly collapse in front of my house— a tradition just to spite my parents—she bends over, gasping for air.

"How much was that? You took a different route, so I know it must be more, right?"

I smile. I'd lied to her. Three miles is our normal distance.

I doubled it today—she was ready.

"Six. Congrats, Briar. You just ran your first 10k."

She gapes at me, and then she punches my arm—*hard*.

"You asshole," she growls. "I thought it felt freakishly hard."

I shrug, still grinning. "You did it, didn't you?"

She blows an exasperated breath through her lips. "Barely."

"How shall we celebrate?" I ask, pulling her waist into my torso.

She wiggles her eyebrows, and I laugh as we sneak into my house and down into the chapel.

After I fuck her on one of the pews, she's quiet as she plays with a piece of hair. I'm stroking her bare stomach, swirling circles around her belly button. She turns her head to the side as her eyes land on random objects in the chapel.

"For so long, I didn't allow myself to think about this— about my future. What it could look like." My fingers still, listening to her words. I could listen to her talk forever. "Samson said something that day, in the woods. Remember? If you have an opportunity to get revenge, wouldn't you?"

I swallow. "And? Did you?" I look at her, fury enveloping me about what was done to her.

She gives me a feline smile. I remember the quad incident—how every interaction with her was met with trepidation. How she recoiled from Hunter the first day I ever laid eyes on her.

"I think so. Now it can all stay in the past. Cam tried so hard to break me that night—both nights. But especially after he escaped. I couldn't breathe. It wasn't until the night he died that I took my first full breath. And guess what?" She smiles as she turns to face me. "I fucking won. He's dead, and I'm alive. I guess that's the best revenge, huh?"

I place her hand on my chest so that she can feel how fast my heart is beating. "You won," I repeat. "That's the *best* revenge."

"You all made it possible," she says quietly.

I shake my head. "No. You did it on your own, baby."

"But you all gave me the courage to believe I could do it myself. Don't you see?"

I pull her on top of me, inhaling the scent of vanilla and honey. I make a promise then and there to show her just how strong she is for the rest of my life. Little does she know, she saved me, too. Gave me the courage to buck my family's history, and consider what I really want to do with my life. I love track, but the more I think about it, the more I want something different for myself. Maybe art school—maybe Boston, to be closer to Silas. Or maybe nothing at all while I figure myself out.

She changed *my* life, too.

I kiss her forehead. "Are you excited for the trip next week?" I ask. The sixty-four students enrolled in senior French are going to Paris for a week—including the five of us.

"So excited." She grins, and her eyes light up. *That* look

—her excitement for the future—burns away all the shadows of her past.

She won.

She fucking won.

❧ 35 ❧

BRIAR

"Give me all the deets," I say, grinning as Jack rolls his eyes. We're all seated on the quad...along with a good chunk of the school population.

Jack sighs. "I met him at Romancing the Bean. Who knew I'd find someone in Greythorn I *hadn't* ever met. He's new—he moved this summer from Georgia. A junior. Into anime," he explains, shrugging. "He's really nice."

"Is Jack Dormand in love?" Ash croons, walking past us.

"Fuck off, Greythorn," Jack says, but they both smile as Ash continues over to a group of students, telling them about a party at his house tonight.

It's as if nothing—and everything—has changed at Ravenwood. Instead of the Kings being hated by everyone, they kind of...blend in now. No one moves when they walk down the hall. No one averts their eyes. It's like the whole thing was a fever dream, and everyone seems to love the newfound lack of hierarchy at Ravenwood.

"That's wonderful. I can't wait to meet him."

"Oh, my god," Scarlett says, laughing from next to me. She points to a group of three guys walking through the gate. "Look at them."

They must be freshmen. I don't think I've ever seen them before, but as they stalk through the quad with menacing expressions, it's clear they want people to know who they are. A few people look at them skeptically.

"Who are they?" I ask as one of them gives me a hard stare.

"The next generation," Hunter muses, putting an arm around me. "I told you. Once our reign fell, someone else would want to swoop in to claim that power."

I twist around and kiss him. When I pull away, I'm nearly laughing. "You poor, poor little dethroned boy."

He shakes his head and looks away.

"I'm going to have to keep an eye on them," Ledger muses, crossing his arms.

"They're just walking. Calm down, everyone." Samson gives me a half smile.

The party that night is different than my first Ravenwood party. Ash especially seems lighter, more himself. He gets people drinks, shows off the art his mother has picked out —thanks to my mom—and he doesn't seem to want to get away from the crowd like he did that first night. Still, I keep my eye on them all as the party wears on. Jack and I dance to the music before he slinks off with his new

AMANDA RICHARDSON

endeavor, and Scarlett is making eyes at some junior girl with long, blonde hair.

As the music dies down, and people begin leaving, I say goodbye to Scarlett and Jack. Hunter offers to drive everyone home, since he stayed sober. I walk them out, and then I turn back to help Ash clean up. Instead, he's grinning at me with my jacket in my arms.

"Let's go."

I roll my eyes and take my jacket as he locks up, leaving the horrifically messy house behind. Thankfully, Ash's mom is on a girl's weekend with my mom. It's sweet —they've really bonded these last few weeks. I'm temporarily breathless as the cold, winter air slams into me. I'll never get used to that feeling. It's like an invisible weight being pressed into my chest. Though I'd never admit that to the guys.

They'd never let me live it down.

"Where are we going this time?" I ask.

"You'll see."

We're quiet as we drive through Greythorn. No music, no talking. It's nearly two in the morning, and the mist is thick against the Edwardian architecture. He pulls into a reserve, driving down a dirt path a couple of miles before coming up to a small shack. It looks abandoned, but the way my skin tingles tells me it was recently occupied.

"Ash," I warn.

He doesn't answer me. Instead, he stops right in front of the dilapidated front door. His eyes find mine a second later.

"Cam lived here."

I grip the edge of my seat. "I don't want to be here—"

"I think you need to let it all out, Briar. This isn't

revenge for me, or Hunter, Ledger, or Samson. This—this is for you."

I give him a warning look, and he laugh. "I know, I know. If you go over there and kick rocks for ten minutes, so be it. But every person needs a chance to get revenge. Do whatever you need to."

Hopping out of the car, I slam the door shut and walk to the front door. At first, I just stand there, jaw clenched. But then something strange happens, and I begin to feel the fury roll through me. The frustration that he took so much of my life, that he violated me, that he betrayed my trust.

But I'm here, and he's not.

I lift my face to the sky, and I scream.

When I'm done, Ash exits the car and walks up to me. He's holding a box of matches and some gasoline.

He grins. "Let's fuck some shit up."

❦ 36 ❧

BRIAR

Paris is everything I hoped for, and more. Though we're chaperoned, Samson manages to cut away from the tour group on our second day. He pulls me into an alley, and I'm breathless with excitement. We emerge onto another street, and throngs of people pass us. The colorful awnings are bright against the grey and white sky, the trees dark and bare from winter.

Everything—I love *everything* about Paris.

The artists along the Seine. The European cars that zoom by on the street. The scent of crepes and falafel. The diversity, the art, the culture...

This is home.

"Where are we going?" I ask, laughing as Samson drags me across the river to Notre-Dame. I pull my jacket close, even though it's warmer here than it is in Massachusetts right now. I look up at the massive stone structure. "I thought it was closed all week?"

"I pulled some strings," he says, smiling. Taking his phone out of his pocket, he speaks to someone in French on the other end.

"Of course you did," I say, feigning annoyance. I am giddy with excitement.

We walk up to the gate, and it's swarming with tourists. Before I realize what's happening, Samson is pulling me through one of the doors to the gothic cathedral.

A security guard nods once, gesturing to a staircase to his right. "You have an hour."

"Thanks, Tom."

Samson pulls me behind him as we ascend a stone staircase. "Who the hell was that and how did you know his name?"

He laughs, tugging me after him—which is good, because despite running three mornings a week, I'm still struggling for air two stories up.

"My uncle knows a lot of people in Paris. He went to culinary school here."

"Ah."

I'm pretty sure all the Kings could pull strings in every city around the world.

We continue to climb, and I have to sit every couple of stories. My legs are burning. Ledger is always talking about cross training, and in this moment, I hate him for being right.

By the time we get to the roof, I nearly collapse.

"Samson," I gasp, but before I have a chance to sling an insult his way, he points to the view.

Every atom in my body stills. Even my breathing regulates in the presence of the magnificent city below me. Not just below me, but out—spreading as far as I can see. The Seine snakes through the center of the city, and I admire the Edwardian buildings, the white stone gleaming in the winter light.

Samson comes behind me, pressing his body into my back. Kissing my head, he holds me. "Beautiful," he says quietly.

"It really is."

"I was talking about you, Briar."

I twist around and wrap my arms around his neck. All the other guys have said *I love you*—except Samson.

I know a part of it is because of Micah.

"This might be the best date you've dragged me on, Samson Hall."

We have a standing date night every weekend, and this one is, by far, the best one yet.

"Which is why I wanted to wait to tell you that I was in love with you. Until I could tell you here, in a place like this."

My breathing hitches as his eyes crinkle around the edges. *God, he's stunning.* And so romantic it sometimes physically hurts.

"I'm in love with you, too," I say quietly, using my tiptoes to kiss his soft lips.

His hands rove down to my jacket, and he unbuttons it one button at a time. I pull away and raise my eyebrows.

"What?" he asks, grinning. "Tell me this wouldn't be the most fun place to have sex."

All the other guys say fuck—but Samson can hardly ever bring himself to say it. I cock my head as I unzip my pants.

"It's cold, so I'm keeping my clothes on."

He growls as he unzips his pants and presses me against the plastic—the only thing between me and my death hundreds of feet below. I swallow.

"Look," he instructs, pointing to the city.

"Fine, you win," I joke, and then I gasp when he enters me, my whole body contracting against him.

"I better win," he rasps, taking my hands and entwining his fingers with mine.

He thrusts into me in a skilled manner—not rough, but enough to pull an orgasm out of me quickly. Undulating against him, he groans as he explodes inside of me, panting as we remain joined together—with Paris spread out below us.

After he cleans me up, we sit and watch the city. I know we'll probably be in a lot of trouble when we rejoin the group, but this was so, so worth it.

"What's going to happen when you go to school here and I'll be in Massachusetts?" he asks quietly, handing me some chocolate.

I bite into the sweet candy. "I don't know. I haven't really thought about it."

He's quiet for a minute. "Is this—are we—" he stops and looks down. "I would understand if this thing—with all of us—was just a casual fling. Something fun to tell your future boyfriend or something."

I look at him, and his eyes find mine. Taking his hand, I kiss it. "How would I ever be able to go back to one guy? My god, it would never, ever compare."

We both laugh, and as we make our way down a few minutes later, I pull him to me in the dark staircase.

"I don't have an answer to your question, by the way," I

murmur. "But I love you all equally, and I don't want to stop what we're doing. Next year may look different, but the five of us didn't get this close for nothing. I think we all share a bond that doesn't come around that often. I'm not going anywhere."

And then I kiss him—deeply. Passionately. Wholly.

The Kings of Ravenwood can have me.

I surrendered a long time ago.

EPILOGUE

Briar

Nine Years Later

"Sweetie, that's a little too high," I croon, trying to keep my voice from sounding as panicked as I feel.

"They have to learn some time," my mom mumbles. Beatrice, my eight-year-old half-sister, is walking Easton, my toddler, along the perimeter of a *very* high play structure.

"He could break his neck," I whine, shifting from foot to foot.

She rolls her eyes, and I guess as a seasoned mother of three, she would know. Blake, my half-brother, is sitting contentedly in the sand, his baby cheeks chubby and pink from the heat.

"I don't understand how you had another one," I joke, crossing my arms. "Easton is a handful."

She smiles and shrugs. "I don't know. I guess I wasn't ready to stop."

"You were almost done raising me! And then Bea came along, and she was older, and bam! Then there was Blake."

She laughs. "I'm going to be sixty-three when he graduates high school."

We break into a fit of giggles. My eyes flick back to Easton. "Careful!"

"Bea has him. Don't worry." She tilts his head. "His hair is getting blonder," she muses, smirking.

I roll my eyes. I'm just about to make a snarky comment when another mom walks over to us.

"Your kids are so cute!" She shields her eyes. "Are they all yours?" she asks me.

I laugh. "Nope. Just the toddler boy. This is my mom, and those are her two kids."

I can see her trying to figure it out—the math, the logistics—but she just nods.

"Hey, babe," Samson says, coming up behind me and wrapping his arms around my stomach. I love when he's in a suit.

"Aw, so sweet. Is this the father?"

My lips twitch with a smile. "One of them."

Her eyes widen, and then she half-walks, half-jogs away.

"You really should stop messing with people like that," Samson purrs in my ear.

I laugh, and my mom smiles as she looks away. "It's so much fun, though."

Two hours later, I hope out of the shower after my run. Checking my phone, I see a picture of Samson and Easton at the museum. I send a quick heart emoji as I pull on a bra and underwear. Slipping into a cocktail dress, I pin my short, light-brown hair up—my mom 'do, as Ash likes to call it. I step into my pumps and grab my purse, exiting my house and climbing into my Porsche. Easton's music begins to blare through the speakers, and I turn it all the way down and place my hands on the wheel.

Sometimes—every few weeks or so—I wish I knew which partner he belonged to. I'm merely curious—I wouldn't necessarily do anything with the information, since they're all so involved in his life. But my mom's comment earlier—about his hair getting blonder...

Three years ago, I went off birth control, and the five of us decided to have a baby. We all got genetic testing, and nothing crazy came up, so we decided to pursue it naturally. We also decided the baby could take a DNA test at any time if we needed any vital medical history, or if he decides he wants to know when he's older.

I got pregnant the first month, and the guys love to joke it's because there are four of them and one of me...

Everyone in our life has been so supportive of our relationship. We have a good system figured out, too. Mondays are Hunter. Tuesdays are Ash. Wednesdays are a free for all...come one, come all. Thursdays are Ledger. Fridays are Samson. Saturday and Sunday are my days to take alone time, run errands, and I have the option of inviting one or some or all of them over. We split childcare evenly, with a similar, rotating schedule for Easton.

Our only rule is that we have to be open about other

relationships. So far, we've all only ever been committed to each other.

The guys each have a separate house in Greythorn—the place we all ended up coming back to. I couldn't imagine leaving my mom, Beatrice, or Andrew, so after four glorious years in Paris, I moved back, got my masters in Boston, and now have my own practice as a therapist. Hunter is working on his sixth book, Ash is the youngest mayor Greythorn has ever had, Ledger is a successful artist, and Samson is an environmental engineer.

I feel lucky most days—overwhelmed, every once in a while—but mostly grateful.

I pull out of my driveway and smile, following directions to a small French place in Boston. Mom life has been a hard adjustment, but having four dads care for our son has helped with *so* much. And it really doesn't matter whose biological son he is. Because really, they all love him equally. I park and walk into the restaurant, excited to see Scarlett and meet her partner. She's in town from New York. Jack is supposed to be here tonight, too. He's in from Miami.

I push the door open, and before I can register what's happening, a bunch of people are shouting at me.

"Surprise!"

"Happy Birthday!"

I nearly fall over and cup my mouth as Hunter descends from the crowd, carrying Easton.

"Hi, sweetie!" I squeal, taking him. It's only been two hours since Samson picked him up, but reuniting with him is my favorite thing in the whole world.

"Mama," he mumbles, wrapping his soft, little arms around my neck. "Ma miss you."

"He did," Hunter muses. "Wouldn't stop saying mama on the car ride home."

I laugh and give him a kiss. "This is incredible," I say, looking around. "Did you plan it?"

"Please," Scarlett interjects, raising her perfectly arched eyebrows. "This was all me."

Hunter chuckles. "It's true." He takes Easton. "Go mingle. Happy Birthday, love."

Scarlett introduces me to her partner, Victoria. They're both chefs in New York. Jack saunters up and kisses me on both cheeks. Though he's still single, he's doing fabulously as a literary agent in Miami. I continue around the room, saying hi to my mom, Andrew, Beatrice, and Blake. I make sure to squeeze Blake as much as I can. The baby chunk gets me every time.

My eyes flit to Ash, who is drinking a beer and talking to Samson. His hair is a bit longer, but the most notable difference is how much muscle he's put on in the last nine years. All the guys really grew into themselves—but Ash especially. Being mayor really had him growing up quickly, and as he smirks at me, I swear I can still see the mischievous glint in his eyes from when we were teenagers. And Ledger, who now has hair tied up into a bun, bends down to kiss me and present me with a bouquet of flowers.

"This is beautiful," I remark, looking around.

"Of course. Did you think we'd forget?"

I laugh. "No, I just—"

"You look beautiful, Briar." Kissing my lips, he trails his finger down my jaw.

"Thank you."

I walk over to Samson, wrapping my arms around his neck. He doesn't need his glasses anymore thanks to Lasik, but I do miss them from time to time. His hair is cut shorter now, and he's always dressed in suits.

"Happy Birthday, little lamb," he whispers.

I give him a peck before walking back to Hunter. Really, I just want to hold my baby.

Hunter gives me a knowing smile as he hands Easton over. He's changed the least—still longer, wavy hair, and stubble. He pulls off the melancholy, tortured writer look very well. It suits him.

"Miss, it's time to be seated," the hostess says, ushering us to a large table. "I wasn't sure which one is your husband, so I—"

I place a hand on her arm. "They all are." Giving her a warm smile, I leave her stunned as I take a seat at the head of the table. I give my mom and Andrew a warm smile, and then I sigh contentedly. On nights like tonight, it's so hard to remember the scared, little girl that first day at Ravenwood. Because without that catalyst—without everything happening the way that it did—my life would be so different now.

Hunter, Ash, Ledger, and Samson all sit surrounding me, with Easton in my lap.

It doesn't matter who is where.

Because they're all here.

And they're all mine.

❧

Thank you so much for reading Ruthless Queen! I truly hope you enjoyed this world and the four Kings. I am planning a spinoff series for some time in 2022, and while I can't go into much detail right now, I am *so excited* to stay in the Ravenwood Academy/Greythorn, Massachusetts world! Please be sure you're subscribed to my newsletter, and perhaps even consider joining my reader group! Those are the two places where I share news first.

MAILING LIST
READER GROUP

If you enjoyed this story, you'd probably like my HEATHENS series—a M/F dark romance. If you enjoy things like taboo priest romance, creepy secret societies, suspense and sexy priests... you'll enjoy HEATHENS and MONSTERS (book 1 and 2).

DOWNLOAD HEATHENS

If you like enemies-to-lovers romance—especially with a TON of steam—you'll probably like Say You Hate Me, my latest office romance.

DOWNLOAD SAY YOU HATE ME

ACKNOWLEDGMENTS

First and foremost, thank you to TikTok for making Ruthless Crown a TOP 50 AMAZON BESTSELLER! I still can't believe that happened—and the day I moved to England, no less. I'll never forget the feeling of landing at Heathrow and seeing a message from a friend with a screenshot that I'd gotten to #42 in the ENTIRE kindle store! It still feels surreal, to be honest. I don't know what I'm doing most of the time on TikTok, but I'm grateful that so many of you found me there!

Second, thank you to my husband because you truly deserve the second spot here. There were many panicked nights before we moved that I wasn't sure I'd finish this book on time, and I spent most of the weeks leading up to our big move behind my computer, trying to make this the best possible story. That meant that you took on our two toddlers by yourself, made dinner, cleaned, and got our lives together enough so that I could write until TWO days before we moved. LOL. I don't base all my heroes on you for no reason. I love you.

Third, to Traci Finlay, who's in-line comments really made editing this story that much more fun. Also, and I always say this, because it's true—this book is a better book because of you. Thanks for your help and for making me laugh while under a tight deadline.

Fourth, to my author friends. I would not be here without your support and encouragement. You inspire me day in and day out.

Fifth, to Give Me Books PR—you guys are amazing, and I have loved working with you on this duet!

To my readers—some of whom have stood by me since I published my first book (a fade-to-black romance, *gasp!*) and are always so, so supportive. But whether you've been here for six and a half years or this is only the second book you've read by me... I appreciate you. You're the reason I continue to do this, the reason I came back after a three year hiatus. I wasn't sure if writing again was a smart or stupid decision at the time, but now I know it happened for a reason. Thank you. For the emails. The comments. The videos. The messages. All of it. Thank you.

And finally, to my kids. I love you both so much, and I hope that one day, mommy can tell you both about how she was able to make her dreams come true.

ABOUT THE AUTHOR

Amanda Richardson writes from her chaotic dining room table in Los Angeles, often distracted by her husband and two adorable sons. When she's not writing contemporary and dark, twisted romance, she enjoys coffee (a little too much) and collecting house plants like they're going out of style.

You can visit my website here: www. authoramandarichardson.com

Facebook: http://www.facebook.com/amandawritesbooks

For news and updates, please sign up for my newsletter here!